A Case for the Toy Maker

A Case for the Toy Maker

An Ainsley McGregor Mystery

Candace Havens

A Case for the Toy Maker
Copyright© 2020 Candace Havens
Tule Publishing First Printing, October 2020

The Tule Publishing, Inc.

ALL RIGHTS RESERVED

First Publication by Tule Publishing 2020

Cover design by Sue Traynor

No part of this book may be used or reproduced in any manner whatsoever without written permission except in the case of brief quotations embodied in critical articles and reviews.

This is a work of fiction. Names, characters, places, and incidents are products of the author's imagination or are used fictitiously. Any resemblance to actual events, locales, organizations, or persons, living or dead, is entirely coincidental.

ISBN: 978-1-953647-05-4

Dedication

To Don and Peggy for always believing.

Chapter One

As I reached up to unlock the back door to my shop, Bless Your Art, something bumped me from behind. "George Clooney, that's rude. Stop it." I turned to find out why he was sniffing me and invading my personal bubble. He was usually well-behaved and courteous—except when squirrels were involved. They were the bane of his existence.

"Oh." Pecans from the pie I'd eaten for breakfast had ended up on my butt. "How did that even happen? Classy, Ainsley." I picked them off and handed them to George who gobbled them up.

I had been kind of groggy from my turkey hangover this morning. I love Thanksgiving, but I have no willpower when it comes to the sides and desserts.

George and I had been worn out by the time we made it home from my friends Shannon and Mike's winery, and we fell asleep on the couch at seven the night before and woke up at five. I'm not normally a morning person, but it was Black Friday, and we had a big day planned at the shop.

After dumping my armful of junk on my desk, I put on a Bless Your Art apron. We'd already decorated for the holidays on Wednesday. I loved that every booth had an individual spin on the holidays, but we'd coordinated with multicolored lights and garland for all the vendors, and we'd draped the walls of the tall brick warehouse in the same way.

The shop was on Main Street, in the middle of Sweet River, Texas, where all the holidays were celebrated by the town with decorations and festivals.

One of which we had coming up soon.

As I reached for the broom, someone banged on the back door. George turned into the demon guard dog, barking loud and ferociously. I may have screamed.

"Ains, are you okay? Are you in there?" my friend Shannon asked.

I laughed nervously, as I unlocked the door. "Did you hear that? I wasn't expecting company."

She held a cardboard container with two cups of coffee. With the other hand, she showed me a brown paper bag. "I have three cinnamon rolls for you and a biscuit for George. I figured you'd need caffeine and sugar to power through today. Do you forgive me for scaring you?"

She owned the coffee shop around the corner and was known for amazing baked goods, and the best coffees and teas in Texas. In the two years that I've lived here, she's become the best friend I've ever had.

"Of, course." I took the bag and the drink. She always brought me an extra one to reheat later in the afternoon. "Thank you."

"I saw you and George drive by and thought, since it's early for you, maybe caffeine would help. Did you hear Jake's coming home tomorrow?"

I snorted. That was the real reason she'd come over. Jake was the local fire chief and a guy I sometimes hung out with. I mean, I thought we were dating. Then, the world went crazy and he headed off to do specialized training for emergency services for three months.

Other than a text or two the first few weeks he was gone, I hadn't heard much from him. Though, he did text me yesterday afternoon to say he was headed home and needed to talk to me.

I'm sure it was to let me down easily, now that he'd be back in town.

Shaking my head, I put all the goodies on the break room table. "Yep. It doesn't matter, it's not like he missed me or I missed him. I mean, sure as a friend but nothing more than that."

Liar.

She scrunched up her face. "Are you sure? He's a tough one to read. Mike said last time he'd talked to him that they were working sixteen-hour days because they'd combined several of the classes."

"He mentioned that to me at the beginning. Not all of us can be you and Mike." I forced myself to grin at her to take the bite from my words. "I've got a lot going on right now. I'm not worried about it."

That wasn't exactly true. Jake was an incredible human being and I cared about him and I'd been certain he had the same feelings for me. But now I wasn't so sure. Distance didn't always make the heart grow fonder.

She chewed on her lip, which meant she wanted to say something. "Okay. I better get back to work—those early morning shoppers need their caffeine."

After she left, I locked the door behind her.

I shook my hands in the air to get rid of the sadness I felt coming on. Nothing would ruin my holiday spirit.

"All right, George. Let's get to work." I leaned down to hug him and he licked me from forehead to chin. "Duuuude. That's so inappropriate."

NINE HOURS LATER, we finally had a lull at the store. There were still kids waiting to see "Santa," who was our favorite toymaker Don, but there were only a few left. We'd been slammed since nine that morning with a store full of customers. It appeared as if everyone wanted to get their holiday shopping done early.

Even though the store was doing okay, we'd had a slow fall, and we were all counting on these holiday sales. That said, I was exhausted and starving. Okay, not starving, but hungry just the same. I needed to get off my feet more than anything. Even with my favorite Skechers, which happened to be a Christmassy red, they were throbbing.

I was about to take a quick break—when an elderly gentleman walked in the door. This guy looked like Santa, even more than Don did, and that's saying something.

Like full-on, white beard, and moustache, but he wore wakeboard shorts with a red sweater that didn't match—and was extremely thin. He smiled and waved at Don, who we'd set up at the front of the store with a throne, backed by several festive Christmas trees.

He'd thought of the idea to keep the kids busy while the parents shopped. And it had worked. We'd also set up a story-time place where we all took turns reading various holiday-themed children's books.

Don grinned and there was nothing but joy on his face.

Who was this guy?

It's probably strange that I was worried about the kids seeing two Santas at once. I never wanted to ruin anyone's fun. But then the kids jumped up and down and yelled, "Two Santas, yeah."

The two of them hugged and it was obvious the guy was a longtime friend. Don glanced at me and waved toward the man. Then he leaned forward to whisper, so the children couldn't hear. "Ainsley, this is my friend Davy Santos. I've known him almost half my life."

"Dude, we are old," Davy said.

They both laughed. It came out as ho, ho, ho, and then kids waiting in line were wide-eyed.

I reached out a hand. "It's nice to meet you." Then it clicked in my head that he was the guy working our Santa house this year. "Um. Santa."

He and Don laughed again.

I was chairperson for our holiday festival, and in addition to running my store, I'd been involved in several committees pulling the event together. It was a ten-day holiday wonderland with vendor booths, a Christmas tree lot, and carnival rides.

It started the next day and I couldn't believe how everything had come together. Six months ago, I wouldn't have thought it possible.

"Yes, ma'am, I'm looking forward to it. I just saw the Santa house, Don. They told me you made it. It's fantastic. I had no idea you and—" Davy glanced around at the children

"—Mrs. Santa were still in town, but I was hoping."

It's hard to tell with Don because his cheeks are always kind of rosy, but I was pretty sure he blushed.

"She's going to have a cow when she sees you. Where have you been?"

Davy opened his mouth, but he was interrupted.

"How come you're a brown Santa and he's a white one? Also, you're kind of skinny," a small black girl asked. She was adorable with her hand on her hip, eyeing the men suspiciously.

Davy knelt down. "Santas come in all the colors of the world and we are all in charge of bringing joy to children." He was sweet about it.

"I thought so," she said. "I have a black Santa book, but I haven't seen one yet."

"Well, now you've seen a brown one. What were you going to ask Santa for?"

She pursed her lips together. "I want the doctor Barbie and a giant dog like that one."

George had peeked around the counter to see what was going on.

This time, we all laughed.

"I'd like to take a break to chat with him," Don said, as he patted his friend on the shoulder. "I haven't seen him in years."

"Of course." Stepping from behind the registers, I grabbed one of the holiday books to read. "Hey kids, the Santas need a lunch break. But I have *Shmelf the Hanukkah Elf* for you."

"Hey, that's my holiday," a boy, who couldn't have been

more than four said. He waved at me. "But we also have a tree 'cuz my dad likes the lights."

"You know what, in Sweet River, we celebrate all the holidays. Everyone is welcome here. And how cool is it that you get to celebrate both holidays?"

"I'm glad we decided to do a big booth together for the Sweet River Holiday Festival," Shannon said, as she finished wiping down the long counter at the front of the booth.

Ours was just outside Bless Your Art at the south end of the big park that ran down the river. There were more than seventy-five booths with all kinds of fun stuff and at the opposite end of the park was the fireman's Christmas tree lot and a bunch of cool carnival rides for kids and adults.

Firemen. Sigh. Don't think about Jake. Too late.

"Are you okay?" Shannon stared at me with a questioning look.

"Yes. Sorry. I was thinking about everything we need to do before we open the festival tomorrow morning."

Ainsley, you've got to stop with the fibbing. You're racking up the wrong sort of Karma points.

"And, me too, on the booth. I think it's natural to pair us together. Your coffee, tea, and hot chocolate—and food—with our artsy stuff. It's going to be great. Also, we're much closer to the store's bathrooms and we don't have to use the Port-o-Potty."

"You said it, sister." She laughed. "We can put people in space and explore new frontiers in the sea—but a chemical toilet that isn't disgusting seems impossible.

"I'm just grateful I don't have to haul those barrels of coffee across the park like last year." Shannon examined her counter. She's OCD about cleanliness, which I find quite endearing.

I especially like it when she organizes my pantry and kitchen cabinets, for real. I'm not a slob, but I'd rather watch holiday movies on Hallmark, than organize anything.

After putting the rag she'd been using back in the cleaning bucket, she turned in a circle. "This could be someone's house. Don and Ms. Peggy did such an amazing job building this."

The booth was something out of a fairy tale. They'd fashioned after the Santa house they'd built, which was in the center of the park. There was gingerbread trim around the roofline and underneath the counter. It was painted white, and we'd used the same lights and decorations we used in the store. Half of it was open with tables and tons of shelving. We were able to put out a great selection of the many items customers might also find in Bless Your Art.

Our festivals, and we had one just about every holiday, pulled in a lot of tourists from all over and we were expecting our biggest year ever. All the B&Bs, campgrounds, hotels, and motels in a sixty-mile radius had been completely booked for months.

"They did," I said. "They finished the Santa house a few days ago. Do you want to check it out with me?"

She nodded.

George had passed out in a corner where we'd stuck one of his old beds under the counter. Technically, he wasn't supposed to be anywhere near food, but we had a special order from the mayor, so he could hang out with me while I worked the booth. "Hey, dude, you want to go for a walk?" In less than a second, he was on all fours.

We laughed.

"If we were at home he would have groaned and given me the stink eye," I said.

We pulled down the flap that closed up the front of the booth, and then we locked the side doors. They'd built it like this so we didn't have to take everything out and bring it back the next day. And the whole thing was movable. We could store it in the old barn at my farm, and load it on a flatbed trailer to take it back and forth to the park for the festivals.

Beat building a new booth every other month for whatever holiday we celebrated. Shannon was right—it was like a mini gingerbread house. I loved it.

After shutting it all down, we headed to the center of the park, waving at friends as we went along. Everyone was doing last-minute prep on their booths. It was chillier than usual, even for late November. We would have great weather over the weekend, but it was supposed to get below fifty tonight.

Funny, being in the fifties and sixties was shorts weather for a lot of people in Chicago, where I'd lived before moving here. Now, even I had a sweater on and was wishing for my coat.

The sun was just above the tree line and with all the Christmas lights on the booths, it was like walking through a winter wonderland.

"There's the Santa house," Shannon said, just as George growled menacingly. "What's wrong, George?"

That growl was never a good sign, and the hairs on the back of my neck stood up.

I had a strong urge to turn around and walk back to the store. But my curiosity knew no bounds. I had to find out what was going on.

We stopped in front of Santa's house, which was a bigger version of our booth except it really did look like a house right out of the North Pole. "Wow, they did a great job. It's fancy," I said.

George growled again. A knot formed in my stomach, twisting hard.

Shannon glanced at him and then me. "Ainsley? You don't think…is something wrong?"

"I hope not," I said. George had done this before and it had never been good news.

He barked and then did the high-pitched whine that told me something I really didn't want to know.

"No," I whispered.

"Ains?"

I took a deep breath and pulled my phone out of my pocket. "Hold on to George—tight." After handing her the leash, I turned on the flashlight app on my phone.

"You're freaking me out," she said, as she gripped the leash tightly.

"I'm freaking myself out." Opening the double doors to Santa's house, I peeked inside.

My breath caught, and bile rose in my throat.

"Call my brother." My voice was nothing more than a

hoarse whisper. I forgot I had my phone in my hand.

"What is it?"

The image of the man with the candy-cane-striped pole sticking out of his chest would be burned in my brain forever.

"Santa is dead."

Chapter Two

"THIS IS A mess," Greg said. He's my brother, and the sheriff. Since we were in the middle of the park, about sixty people had gathered behind the crime-scene tape, all of them trying to get a peek at Dead Santa.

A shiver coursed through my body. Poor Davy. I'd only met him for a few minutes, but he seemed like a genuinely nice person. That, and he was a friend of Don's, who was one of the best men I know.

The crime-scene techs combed the inside of the house, and Kane—a friend and also the medical examiner—had just moved the body to the morgue. Normally, I'd be the one with a million questions, but that pole in his chest—it was just such a violent way to die.

I lifted my head to find my brother glancing my way.

"It's not my fault." I crossed my arms. Shannon and I sat on some folding chairs just outside the crime-scene perimeter.

Holding her arms around her belly, she rocked gently. It was tough seeing a dead body. For me, even though I'd been through this a few times, it never was any easier.

I had a lot of respect for the officers and CSI folks who did this sort of thing for a living. Mentally, I wouldn't be able to handle it. Even though George and I had found a few dead bodies in the past. Still, it was just as big of a shock the third time, as it was the first.

"I never said you did," Greg said. "Stay here just a minute; we need to get your statements."

I nodded.

"Are you okay?" I asked Shannon.

Shannon shook her head. "It's surreal. Like, did I really see what I thought I saw? I can't quite comprehend it."

Yes. Santa on his throne with the North Pole sticking out of his chest—it was the thing of Christmas nightmares.

"I'm sorry?" I didn't really know what to say. I felt bad that she had to go through this. She's a tender soul who feels the weight of the world in her heart.

"Don't be. I'm glad you weren't alone this time." Then she sniffed.

We hugged each other, holding on tight, as if we were trying to give the other one strength. It really did hurt my heart that she'd stepped up and peeked over my shoulder. She was such a kind soul.

Her optimism was one of the things I adored most about her but right now she looked as though the world might never be right again.

Greg came back, with my not-so-favorite person, Deputy Investigator Lucy, with her perfect ponytail and judgment in her eyes. For some reason, she didn't like me much and I had no idea why.

She'd been there the first time I found a dead body, and was so judgey when she interviewed me. That she made me feel guilty, when I'd done nothing, was something I'd never forget.

She wore a dark blue suit jacket with dark jeans, and a white shirt. In the television world, she could play the hotshot detective, who always managed to be put together.

"Okay, I think you remember Lucy—she's going to take your statements," Greg said.

Oh. Joy.

Lucy held out a hand, and Shannon and I each shook it. "You two doing all right? That had to be a shock. Not sure I'll be able to get that image out of my head anytime soon," she said.

Wait. She's being nice?

"I didn't do it. It's George's fault," I blurted out. I don't know why she made me nervous. There are some people who are just intimidating and she was one of them.

She sat down in the chair across from us. "I'm not here to accuse you of anything," she said softly. This was not at all like the last time I'd talked to her. "I just need to know a few things. Okay?"

Shannon and I nodded.

"Right. Ainsley, you go first." She pointed her pen at me. "Tell me what happened from the time you left your booth, until you found the body."

I closed my eyes. It helps me think and see things as they happened. I have no idea why.

"We were just taking George for a walk and checking out the festival booths. There were lots of people around. When we were close to Santa's house, George growled. He does that when—uh—bad stuff happens.

"I peeked inside, and, yeah. It was dark. None of the lights were turned on. I used my flashlight on my phone. At first, I didn't see anything. Then, there was the pool of blood on the floor. I smelled the coppery scent. I just knew. And I moved my phone a bit to see how big the puddle was and noticed his boot. Then I followed it up. I thought maybe he'd fallen asleep in there.

"And the North Pole was sticking out of his chest. His eyes were wide as if he'd been surprised. And there were a bunch of candy canes stuck in his mouth."

I took a deep breath to steady my nerves. My hands wouldn't stop shaking. "I didn't walk in because it was obvious he was dead, and I didn't want to contaminate the crime scene. And then I asked Shannon to call Greg. I forgot I had my phone in my hand. I just couldn't believe what I'd seen." I opened my eyes. And let out a breath I hadn't realized I'd been holding.

"That was smart of you." Her pen paused on the pad she'd been writing on. "You said you were close, so he started growling before you were in front of the house?"

"Yes. We were probably twenty feet south of here, and he jerked toward the left and sounded really mean. Like he was trying to protect me from someone."

She leaned forward. "Did you see anyone? Maybe behind the stalls?"

I shook my head. "I was looking down at George, trying to figure out what was wrong with him."

"Did you hear anything?"

"No. Like I said, I was focused on my dog."

"I did." Shannon spoke up. "I mean, I know it's not my turn to talk, but my story is exactly the same except for one thing."

We both stared at her. I had no idea what she was about to say.

"It's okay, tell us." Lucy's voice was soft and encouraging.

This was a new version of the surly investigator I'd never encountered before.

Greg had been motioning to the crowd to move back. Probably to make sure no one overheard us. It would be bad enough keeping the rumors at bay. Our town was known for its expert gossipers. Nevertheless, they did what he asked.

His men took over, and he walked closer to where I sat with Shannon.

"When George lunged, I glanced between the stall behind us and Santa's house," Shannon said. "I can't tell you what made me look that way. Maybe it was the direction he pulled Ainsley.

"There was a shadow cast by the Christmas lights. But it was at an odd angle. I can't tell you if it was a man or a woman, but it was a bulky shadow. Kind of wide." She spaced out her hands as if she measured a fairly stout person. "But that's the only difference."

Her hand shook as she pulled the blanket they'd given her tighter around her shoulders.

"Anything else?" Lucy asked.

"No." Shannon sniffed. "It's really cold out here. I can't stop shaking."

I hugged her and wrapped my blanket around her as well.

"You're in shock. We'll get you inside. I just have one more quick question," she said as she stood. "Did either of you know the victim?"

"No," Shannon said.

"Sort of." I waved my hand.

"Please explain," the detective said, but not in the snotty way she had when I'd first met her. Something was different about her and I needed to remember to ask my brother. "He came into the shop today. He'd an old friend of Don's. They seemed really happy to see each other."

"Don?"

"He has a booth at my shop. He and his wife, Peggy, built this Santa house. The guy came in, and then they walked back to the break room. I got the feeling they hadn't seen each other in a long time. That's the only time I saw him."

Lucy pursed her lips. "Did you hear a name?"

"Davy." What was his last name? I replayed the scene in my head. "Davy Santos. I remember, because he's the one the festival committee hired to play Santa for us."

"We should get you two inside." Lucy closed her notebook. "I'd suggest getting checked out by the paramedics. You both look like you're in shock." She handed us each a card. "If you think of anything else, a sound or someone who seemed out of the ordinary as you were walking by, don't hesitate to call. Sometimes, after a good night's rest, your mind will clear and the details become finer."

I hoped that didn't happen. The last thing I wanted to remember better was that scene. In fact, I was determined to purge it from my brain. They had my statement.

I glanced at Greg, who walked up and then stood next to Lucy. "I'm sending one of Jake's EMTs to check you out at the shop. Lucy is right. You may both be suffering from shock."

Just like my brother to listen to every word, even though it hadn't looked like it.

I was just glad to get away from there. There'd been a lot of blood and that coppery scent had flooded my nose. I needed a hot shower, and maybe some peppermint oil to get the smell out.

We tried to hand the blankets back to Greg. He'd pulled them out of the back of his SUV for us. "Keep them," he said.

"Does Kane have a cause of death, yet?" I asked him.

His eyebrow went up. "The large hole in his chest from the North Pole sign was probably the culprit." The side of his mouth twitched like he was trying not to grin. It might seem rude to other folks, but for police officers and those who dealt with this sort of thing, humor was the one thing that got them through. It wasn't a disrespect for the dead. More a survival instinct.

"Ha. Ha. I meant, did someone do it to him, or did he do it to himself?"

"Kane's running toxicology and a bunch of other tests. He could have stumbled and impaled himself and then fallen back in the chair, but it's unlikely. We'll know more in a few hours."

"All right."

"Ains?"

"What?"

"If I ask nicely, will you stay out of this?"

"As long as you don't go around arresting my friends."

That had happened more than once. "Right now, all I can think about is a hot shower."

"Me, too," Shannon agreed.

"Poor Don." I put an arm around Shannon, as we walked back to my store.

"I know," Shannon said. "Maybe we should check on them later," she said as we entered the warmth of Bless Your Art.

"He'd said he hadn't seen his friend in years and he's going to be sad when he finds out what happened." I brought my shoulders to my ears to relieve the tension there.

Maybe it was an accident. I mean, I'm a full-on klutz most of the time. It's why I don't have sharp edges or anything that I could impale myself with in my house.

George is the same way. Great Danes are huge but not terribly graceful most of the time.

But my spidey senses said there was no way this was anything but murder.

Sometimes I really hated my spidey senses.

Chapter Three

SHANNON AND I were in my office, where I grabbed my scarf and wrapped it around my neck. Then I picked up my purse and backpack to head home.

We'd been given the once-over by a couple of EMTs. They suggested we have someone drive us home so we could rest. But we were fine.

Well, as much I could be.

"Do you want to borrow a jacket? I have a couple of extras here. I'm always forgetting mine."

"I don't think I'll ever be warm again."

I wrapped myself up in a green fuzzy jacket that was a size too small—maybe two at this point. I'd eaten a lot of turkey the day before.

"It will be okay. You're looking grayish. I can run you by the emergency room."

She blew out a breath. "Nah. The EMT said this sort of shock is normal. I just need a hot shower and Mike. He's texted me about eleventy hundred times the last half hour."

I chuckled. Her fiancé was protective in a sweet way, as in she was his queen and he would do anything for her. I'd be hard-core jealous of their relationship, if I didn't love them so much.

"Well, let's get you home. I'll drop you off on the way to

my place, or are you staying at your place?" She had an apartment above her coffee shop, but she'd been spending most of her time out at Mike's vineyard. That's where she'd be living full-time once they were married next June.

"I want to go to Mike's, but don't you think we should drop by Don's and pay our respects? I mean, you said that man was his friend."

I stopped short of the back door, my keys jangling in my hand. "I'm sure the police need to notify Davy's family first."

She gave a wry half smile. There was a hundred percent chance Don and Peggy already knew through the Sweet River grapevine. I only hoped whoever told them had done it gently. Most folks probably had no idea the victim was friends with them.

"Lucy's eyes kind of lit up when you mentioned Don knew the Santa. I bet they head there soon."

I nodded. "I shouldn't have said that. Poor Don. She better not jump to conclusions."

"Well, if she does, maybe we should go ahead and talk to Don."

"Shannon, are you suggesting we talk to Don to find out what he knows? I promised I'd stay out of this one."

She glanced down at her adorable knee-high boots. "Do you think it was an accident? I never met the man, but he didn't deserve that."

I bit the inside of my lip. "I don't know." I sighed. "But Lucy and her team will be interviewing Don and Peggy tonight. I'm still mad at myself for selling him out."

"You didn't. There was no other way you could explain how you met him."

She was right, but guilt still weighed heavy on me. Don and Peggy were two of my favorite people in the world. When I'd been in the hospital, they were some of my first visitors and Peggy worked with the others at Bless Your Art to make sure the store was always covered and that I was fed.

They'd also been there for me during the planning stages of Bless Your Art.

I owed them a lot.

"If she or my brother sees me anywhere near—"

"You'll get in trouble?"

It was the first time in an hour the tightness in my chest let loose. There was a reason she was my best friend. "But we aren't investigating. We're just paying our respects, okay? They seemed to have been really good friends and I'm sure they are hurting."

She chewed on her lip. "Okay."

Just then my phone dinged. It was Don. He texted: *Need to chat tonight. Come soon.*

"Or maybe we should go tonight." I showed her my phone.

She nodded solemnly.

"What if he's mad that I blurted out about him being friends with the victim?"

"You know he wouldn't care. The police would have found out eventually. What if we get a shower and change? And then maybe take some food over around seven. We won't stay long. I mean, it's not butting in if he asked you."

That would give Lucy and my brother time to chat with Don first and they wouldn't be able to accuse me of butting in.

"True."

Color bloomed on her cheeks. That was a good sign. "I have a couple of quiches I need to grab from the shop. That gives me a good excuse to come with you. Plus, if he *is* mad, I can defend you."

She was the best friend ever.

"I have a leftover pecan pie from yesterday." One that hadn't landed on my butt. Man, Thanksgiving seemed like it was a hundred years ago, not twenty-four hours. Interesting how fast life changed.

I bet poor Davy had no idea he'd die so violently when he woke up this morning.

Why would anyone kill a Santa Claus? I mean, if it was a murder.

But how did he get back on this throne?

My heart hurt for Davy and his family. That smile of his had been infectious.

I frowned.

"What are you thinking about?"

"That poor Don lost someone he cared about today. We need to remember that."

She closed her eyes and took a deep breath. "You're right."

Two hours later, Shannon and I arrived at Don and Peggy's ranch. They had more than a hundred acres with a dairy farm, and sheep. The wool from the sheep was used to make yarn. Lucrative businesses—that other people ran for them. Still, I'd never seen a retired couple who worked harder than these two.

Don's big passion was making toys of all types. He made things out of wood, iron and other metals. And they weren't bulky block-like things, though he did have that sort of thing for infants. His were more sophisticated toys with moving pieces.

People came from all over for his train cars. He had an elaborate setup in the shop, and had built a Christmas village around it for the season.

For the holidays, he also created sets, and figurines. As far as I knew, he could make just about anything.

And Peggy—she was a DIYer who was more comfortable with a jigsaw and planer than most men. They created things together, like the booths at the festival, and never a harsh word was spoken. They were the ideal couple, and had something that I hoped to find one day.

"There's no one else visiting," Shannon said as we pulled up in front of the modern farmhouse. "I thought half the town would be here by now."

I pointed down the drive to where the barn was. There were at least six cars parked outside of it.

"Oh," she said. I drove around the side of the house and pulled up in front of the big green barn. The doors were open and all the lights were on.

The cars were very familiar.

"Looks like the crew from Bless Your Art is here. I guess the Sweet River grapevine has struck again. Poor Don and Peggy."

"I kind of hoped we'd be the only ones. But if the police

came out here, people would be curious as to why."

Nothing went unnoticed in this town.

We grabbed the food from the back of my SUV, and carried it into the barn.

I'd only been out here a couple of times, when I'd been talking to Don about opening a booth in my shop almost two years ago.

The couple had stopped by when I'd been outside the building with the architect. When they learned about the sort of artist co-op I wanted to create, they were all in. And they brought along some talented artists from all over the county with them.

In the barn, everything was neatly organized on shelves that covered the walls of the structure from the floor to the ceiling. There had to be thousands of toys. But there was a kitchen area, with a long quartz island and a bunch of barstools at the far end.

My friends and vendors at the shop—Mrs. Whedon, the Queen of Knitting; Maria Federline, my favorite cross-stitcher; and Pete, who made medieval weapons and the most delicate glass Christmas ornaments—sat around the large island talking. They'd all been at the store when Davy had been there.

Maybe the rest of the town didn't know yet that Don was a friend of the victim. But it wouldn't be long.

"I had a feeling we'd see you tonight." Don smiled as we sat the food on the countertop. But tonight, that winning grin of his didn't make it to his eyes.

"I'm sorry for your loss," I said, and I meant it.

"My heart hurts for you," Shannon added. "I don't know

what I'd do if I lost one of my friends."

"Thank you, both. I appreciate it." His voice was husky with emotion.

Poor Don. I blinked to keep from tearing up.

"We brought you some quiches and some pies," I said. "Do you want me to take them up to the house? Where's Ms. Peggy?"

He shook his head. "Nah. I'll put them in the fridge here. This time of year, we cook most of our meals in here. We're both always working on a project. And my better half is with the volunteers decorating the nursing home.

"You know how she is, can't sit still for long. After the police were here, she was all tied up in knots. We can't believe what happened. She said she needed to get out and do something cheerful. I offered to go with her, but she told me to stay here in case there was more news. I always do what she says." He put the things away.

He wasn't lying about the doing what she said. It was probably how their marriage had survived for so many years. That, and I'd never met a more easygoing soul than Don.

"Did you guys come for information?" His jovial tone was gone, but he wasn't mad.

"We just wanted to pay our respects, I promise." And I meant it. "I can't believe we just met him and he's gone. He seemed like such a nice man, and he'd been excited to see you. That was evident the minute you two saw each other."

He patted my shoulder, much the same way he'd patted Davy's earlier. "Do you want anything to eat or drink?" He motioned to the island, which was piled with food.

"We're good," Shannon said.

"I was just about to tell everyone how we met; take a seat. I thought maybe talking about him with you guys might help me remember something from earlier today." He sat on a stool on the other side of the island.

"Have you already told the police what you're going to say to us? I don't want to get in trouble again."

He nodded. "They left about a half hour ago."

Whew. At least, I didn't have to worry about running into Greg or Lucy.

"I met Davy at a convention for Santa Clauses in Minnesota. That's were Peg and I used to live before we moved here. Gosh, that's maybe twenty-five years ago? I can't remember exactly. It was our last winter up north, and we'd already bought this place, but we couldn't move until Peg finished her last semester teaching at an elementary school there."

I leaned forward on the counter, taking it all in. I'd had no idea she'd been a teacher.

"I'd retired from my job as an engineer the year before, but I was bored. And even back then I had the beard, and the belly. I looked into playing Santa Claus and that's how I ended up at my first convention with Davy. We met at the Santa's Laughter Workshop."

We all chuckled.

He waved a hand. "I know, it sounds crazy. But if you're too loud, or gruff, it can scare the tiny ones. It's something you have to know how to do and practice until it comes from deep down. The instructor said it was the sound of joy, and I don't disagree."

He stared down at the coffee cup he held between his

hands. "Anyway, that's where we met. We kept cracking each other up and breaking character, which is a big no-no in our business. If you're wearing the suit, no matter what is going on, you stay in character. I know that now, but like I said, I was new to it then. Our instructor kicked us out, and we ended up in the pub downstairs."

Don stared down at his laced fingers. "We got to talking, like you do over a couple of beers. And he'd mentioned he'd retired, too. He didn't tell me what from, and I don't think I ever asked. He'd lived all over the place, and didn't like to stay anywhere for long. Said he got bored and liked making new friends."

He paused. "He was one of the nicest guys I've ever met. Like, went out of his way to do kind things for folks. Right after we met him, Peggy had to have surgery. Davy brought food over at least two or three times a week. I can cook, but he could have been a chef. Peggy swore his chicken and dumplings made her heal faster."

I had a soft spot for kind people. There just weren't enough of them in the world.

"We lost contact a couple of years ago. We used to at least get a Christmas card from him. I'd done a couple of internet searches to see if I could find him, but never had much luck. He's one of those people who doesn't do social media or anything like that.

"After a while, I thought maybe he'd died while traveling. Even though I couldn't find an obit. Broke my heart. But then—he showed up in the store earlier today. For me, it was like seeing a ghost. I'd never been so happy to see a face. Peggy and I were excited to have him out to dinner tonight.

I'd even asked him to come stay with us."

I cleared my throat. "Did he say why he applied to be our Santa for the festival?"

Don uncrossed his fingers. "Funny enough, he had no idea Peg and I were still here. He was excited to see me when he walked into the store. Someone on Main Street had told him the real Santa was at Bless Your Art."

"I wondered how he'd found you."

"Davy said he had a feeling, especially since this was our last address. He was hoping we were still here. But he'd lost our contact info when he'd dropped his phone on a trip two years ago. He had to come check out Bless Your Art to see if it might be me. I didn't even know what to say at first but then in minutes it was like we'd never been apart."

And now he was dead. My gut tightened again, and tears burned in my eyes, more for Don's loss than anything.

"Goodness," Shannon sniffed. Evidently, I wasn't the only one affected by his story. "That makes me even more upset for you and Ms. Peggy."

He gave us a sad smile. I glanced around. Everyone was unusually quiet for our crew. "Do you know anything about what happened?" he asked. "Your brother was kind about it and that woman with him. But they couldn't comment on an ongoing investigation. But I heard you two were the ones who found him."

If I said something, someone in this group would snitch. Not that they'd do it on purpose—it's just how folks were in this town. They always say small towns are full of secrets, but I'm not sure about Sweet River. Pretty much everyone knows everybody's business.

"Safe, circle?" I made eye contact with each one of them. "If Greg finds out, you guys know better than most what he'll do to me." Technically, nothing. But I didn't want to listen to him nag. Ever since that one time, when I almost died—again—he's been such a mother hen.

Mrs. Whedon, who wore a fluffy avocado jacket with tracksuit pants, held up her fingers in the Boy Scout salute. I'm pretty sure that didn't count if you weren't a part of that organization. The others followed suit.

"Not a word, to anyone outside this barn, got it?"

They all nodded, including Shannon.

"They don't know if it was an accident or a murder. I don't want to get too graphic, and Kane is running a bunch of tests, but there was an object in Davy's chest, and we found him on the throne in Santa's house at the festival. There was a lot of blood. George sensed it before we did—that's why we opened the doors to look inside. And I promise that's all I know."

"And I saw a big shadow," Shannon said. "But I didn't see who it was."

"But you're going to find out more, right?" Don asked, his soulful Santa eyes seeing straight through to my heart. "You'll check with Kane and keep us informed? Your brother is a good man but he's got his hands full these days. And I trust you. I'm a nice guy but I don't say that to many people. I'm asking for your help to make sure that we know exactly what took place. If something terrible happened to your friend, wouldn't you do anything in your power to find out what the story was?"

I sighed, and then nodded. Who was I to tell Santa no?

Chapter Four

THE NEXT MORNING, I parked in my spot at the back of the store. It was early. I had a big day ahead with the festival. Luckily, this town was full of volunteers who were happy to take most of the load when it came to checking on vendors to make sure they were okay.

But I'd come in early because I had to make sure the store was ready, and I hadn't been able to sleep the night before. Don's stories about his friend, Davy, made the man all too real for me. And like Shannon, my heart hurt for those he'd left behind.

Then there was the fact that Don had asked me to look into things. I love that old man. He's like the grandpa I never knew and I wouldn't disappoint him.

"No one looks better in a Santa hat than you do, George Clooney." I smiled, as I fitted the elastic band around his floppy ears. "Now, don't do your slobber shake, and that should last all day. Besides, the last time you did that in Bless Your Art, you stained Mrs. Whedon's yarn and she still hasn't forgiven you."

George sighed. He really was the perfect man—other than the drooling problem—and the best four-legged friend a woman could have.

Then he grinned.

"Santa hats are cool, but not the *Jaws* doggie costume for Halloween." He'd seemed particularly mortified when I put that outfit on him, and then promptly sulked on the couch for the rest of the party.

"Woof!"

"I don't blame you, George," a deep and familiar voice said behind me. I might have jumped and screamed a bit (okay, it was a lot of screaming) until I realized who it was—Jake—the local fire chief and the guy I'm not sure I'm dating.

And in my defense, more than one person has tried to kill me. It was seven in the morning and I didn't think anyone else would be around.

He held up his hands in surrender. "It's just me."

"You scared me to death," I said, as I leaned on George as if he were a lifesaver, the kind that floats, not the candy. But then the traitor ran to Jake, nearly knocking the giant of a man down.

My breath caught in my throat and it had nothing to do with the fright—and everything to do with Jake in a Henley, dark jeans, and boots. This guy was more handsome than Chris Hemsworth and he had scruff on his jaw. I'm a sucker for some scruff.

It wasn't fair for him to look good—especially this early in the morning. Meanwhile, I was dressed in sweats that belonged to my brother. My hair was in a messy ponytail and I had the oldest pair of sneakers I owned on. They were also the most comfortable. I brought clothes to change into for when we opened the shop but those were hanging in the back of my car.

Unfortunately, he'd seen me look worse when I'd nearly been killed a few months ago, and landed in the hospital.

And I'm not even sure if he sees me as attractive. I mean, we went on two of what I'd call real dates. And then he left town for several months for the fire chief training.

Like I'd told Shannon, I'd received a couple of texts. And he called me on my birthday and sent some flowers. But everything had been sort of awkward and I wasn't sure why.

Yep. My relationship with Jake was complicated.

He knelt down and hugged George's neck. "What a good boy you are."

The dog showered him with kisses, and Jake laughed hard. "Yuck, George, we've talked about this. I appreciate the love but I'm not into PDA."

Funny and gorgeous—have I mentioned how unfair it was?

"When did you get back to town?" my voice squeaked.

Get a grip, Ainsley. It's just Jake.

"About an hour ago. I stopped by the station to pick up some paperwork that had stacked up." He petted George while we talked, and the traitor stared up at Jake adoringly.

Who am I to judge? I have to remind myself not to drool when he's around.

"Austin was good?" Look at me with the idle chitchat—and I almost sounded normal. But this was awkward.

"It was. I came back with a whole lot of ideas on how to streamline our emergency services."

That sounded very important. "Cool. You were gone a long time." Wait. Did I say that out loud? Darn.

He chuckled. "I was. I'm sorry I haven't been great about

calling you. It was a rough couple of months. I planned to see you today, but then I saw you drive by the station, and it's early. I thought maybe your alarms had gone off and I didn't want you to go in there by yourself."

Well, at least he cared about my safety. Though, that probably had to do with the fact I'm the sister of his best friend—Greg.

"Nah. I'm okay. Just thought I'd come in early to get ready. The festival starts today." I'm sure he knew that, but thinking of things to say that weren't: What happened? You told me you liked me—was becoming increasingly difficult.

And, yes. I'm a grown woman. I usually don't have a problem with saying what I need to, but this was Jake. We were friends first—and I didn't want to jeopardize that by being too clingy or needy.

"Ah. Well. I just wanted to make sure you were okay."

"Yep. All good."

He gave George another chin rub. "Well, I won't keep you." He started to walk away.

I blew out a breath I didn't realize I'd been holding. "Hey, Jake?"

He stopped and turned around, giving me that smile of his, sending my heart on some kind of wild adventure in my chest. "Yes?"

I smiled back. "I'm glad you're home."

His grin grew. "Me, too, Ains. Can we talk later?"

At least, there was that. He was such a nice guy, he'd probably been worried about letting me down easy.

"Sure."

"And do you mind if I come get George later? The guys

wanted to play flag football this afternoon."

Well, I guess George was still dating Jake—just not me. It's not like I have some claim to him. Jake, not George. "Of course."

～

STOP THINKING ABOUT him. *You have work to do.*

Thank goodness for my conscience.

After opening the back door, I let George go in first. Ever since someone tried to kill me a few months ago, everything seemed spookier than it really was. I flipped on the lights and then locked the back door.

"I'm lucky I have the best guard dog ever."

George woofed and I laughed. He made me do that a lot, which was one of the many reasons I loved him.

Who needed a handsome fireman when I had all the unconditional love I could handle from my four-legged bestie?

He followed me into the office where I flipped on all the electronics and hooked up the holiday playlist I'd put together. My plan was to dump my stuff, make sure everything was ready to start the day in the booth and the store, and then text Kane to see if he was working.

I'd promised my brother I'd stay out of this. But Don was upset about his friend. The very least I could do was find out exactly how he died. Besides, the Bless Your Art crew had become family to me. We had such a great group and when I needed them, they were there for me. There was no way I'd let Don down.

My brother was right about the obvious answer, but one

never knew. And I have this innate curiosity that gets me in trouble a lot. I couldn't really control it. I had to know what happened to Davy. How odd that the man was killed just hours after reuniting with this best friend. The timing was off.

Do not let your mind go there. Don and Peggy were not suspects. They'd been home waiting for Davy to come over for dinner. But Don had been in the Santa house. What if he wanted to stay one step ahead of the police and that was why he wanted me to find out what was going on?

Ainsley!

I bit my lip. This was dumb. Don was a kind and gentle soul.

George barked just as the back door opened and Don walked through.

"Hey, George!" He pet him and then leaned down so George could nuzzle his beard a bit.

And you think he might be a killer.

Don frowned and then smiled when he saw me in the office doorway. "Hey, you're here early."

"Big day," I said. "Is something wrong? I thought you'd be taking off today, given what's happened."

His eyebrows drew together. "Peggy is right. Sitting around is not good for us. I keep thinking if I'd just hung around a little longer or made him come home with me right then, he'd still be alive."

The anguish on his face pulled at my heart. Poor guy.

"You can't know that. And there's no sense blaming yourself."

"That's what Peggy said. Still, I wish I'd made him come

home with me when I left. He said he had some folks to talk to and then he'd be there in a bit."

"Did he mention if they were male or female?"

He scratched his chin as he thought about it. "I don't think so. I'm pretty sure he said *folks*. He was super excited about the house. Told me it was the nicest one he'd ever worked in."

I hadn't wanted to grill him the night before. But there was a chance Davy might have mentioned something to him.

"I know you probably told my brother everything, but I'm curious if he said anything to you in the break room. You guys were in there for an hour."

Don puffed out a breath. "I'd asked him where he'd been the last two years and if he'd been back to Minnesota. He said he'd been making toys and lamps with a friend of his. I got a feeling it was a woman, just by the way he was talking about her."

"Did it seem like he was upset about anything?"

Don shook his head. "It was the opposite. He said he'd never been happier. That his life had taken a good turn. His health wasn't the best. We didn't get into that much. In true Davy style, he didn't talk that much about himself. He asked a lot of questions about my life. That was it. Then we chatted a bit when I was finishing the interior lights in the Santa house. But it was more about the structure."

Don sniffed. "I know I haven't seen him for years, but he's a good guy, Ainsley. Or, he was. Just salt of the earth; do anything for a friend. I can't imagine anyone wanting to hurt him."

I cleared my throat. "Well, I will find out what I can.

Like I said last night, I promised my brother I'd stay out of it. But I have my resources. We'll figure this out."

At least, I hoped so.

After finishing up at the shop, and checking that we were ready to roll with the booth, I texted Kane. He was one of those people who woke up at four to go jogging and to workout. I've never understood people who do that. I mean, the trails and the gym equipment are there after ten in the morning. Why kill yourself waking up early?

Kane said he was headed to get coffee, so I decided to meet him at Shannon's shop.

"Ainsley McGregor, you are up early two days in a row. Are you running a fever?" Shannon leaned over the counter to put a hand to my forehead.

I may have rolled my eyes. "Big day today."

"True. Are you doing okay after yesterday?" she whispered as she washed her hands.

"I'm okay. How about you?"

She scrunched up her face. "I had a really hard time sleeping last night. Every time I closed my eyes, I saw—yeah. I mean, you've seen more than your share, but I hope that never happens again."

I pursed my lips. "It's not something you ever get used to, I don't think. Unless maybe you're my brother or Kane, and it still affects them but they've learned to separate themselves from it. I'm sure it takes years to be able to do that."

"Are you talking about me?" a deep baritone voice said from behind me.

This time I didn't jump. I turned to greet Kane, who is a

doppelganger for a young Idris Elba. I'm not even kidding. We had more than our fair share of incredibly handsome men in this part of Texas.

Today, he wore a dove-colored button-down, with jeans and cowboy boots. Handsome as ever, it was his blue eyes that drew me in every time. They were kind and compassionate—which, given the nature of his job, was nothing short of a miracle.

He has a girlfriend.
Doesn't mean I can't appreciate how handsome he is.

"Hey." I reached my arms out to hug him. "Did you have a good Thanksgiving?"

He hugged me and then waved at Shannon. "We did. My grandmother kept refilling my plate. I'm pretty sure I fell asleep at the table, and when I woke up, she was still feeding me."

We all laughed.

"Do you guys want your regulars?"

Kane and I nodded.

"I'll get them ready for you—uh—just wait for me, please?" she asked. "I know it's none of my business, but since I was there—I'd like to know what happened."

Kane's brow furrowed and then he smirked. "I thought we were just catching up?"

"Well, we were talking to Don last night. He's sad, Kane. He was friends with the victim for more than a quarter of a century. Shannon and I promised we'd look into things for him, and for Peggy."

Kane shook his head. "When your brother said you wouldn't be butting into this one I had a feeling he was wrong. You found the body and you have a natural curiosity about these things."

"True. But we also promised Don. He's like the grandpa of the shop. Can you tell your grandmother no?"

"You got me there."

"Please, wait for me," Shannon said. "Ben can cover for me for a few minutes."

Kane sighed dramatically. "You're going to get me in trouble."

"Thank you," I said. "I knew I could count on you."

Shannon stared at us expectantly.

Kane shook his head but then grinned. "She's going to tell you as soon as I leave. I guess it will be okay."

He and my brother tried to keep me out of the loop, the first time this happened, but I still found out everything I needed to by doing my own investigation. Also, I'd helped catch the killer—twice—even though the last time that terrible woman almost murdered me.

I hadn't been solving murders for long and I sometimes didn't figure things out until it was almost too late.

Kane and I had become great friends. And, unlike my brother, he respected my opinion. We sometimes discussed his cases in a hypothetical way and he liked that I didn't always look at the world the same way everyone else did.

I'm not sure what he meant by that, but if it gave me insider info, I was okay with it.

We sat down at the table nearest the window, and away from the morning crowd. Normally, we'd be in his office, where it was way more private. But I'd do anything to avoid visiting the morgue. That disinfectant they use—it's just not a pleasant smell mixed with death.

"How is Eva?"

Kane had been dating her for a couple of months. If ever there was a doctor power couple, it was those two. They were perfect for one another.

He stared out the window. "Uh. We're taking a break," he said. His eyebrows knit together.

"Oh. I'm sorry. I didn't know."

He clasped his hands. "Happened about a week ago."

"Are you okay?" The last time I'd seen them together was at my Halloween party in October. He'd stared at Eva lovingly. I couldn't imagine him letting that go.

"I'm committed to my job and so is she. But we tried to talk about the future and it all—She asked me to marry her," he said, as if that answered everything.

Wow. Eva was a woman who went after what she wanted. I admired that. As much as I like to think I'm strong, no way I'd ever do that with Jake.

Part of me thought that if I just asked Jake outright what was going on, he'd break up with me. Which was kind of silly, since I wasn't sure we were actually dating. I didn't want to lose him as a friend and it just seemed easier to avoid talking about everything.

It was like I was back in high school.

"And you said no?"

"Not exactly." He continued to stare out the window and I sat back in my chair. We were great friends and it made me happy that he felt like he could tell me something like this.

"I'm confused. Did she change her mind?"

He shook his head, and focused on me. "No. I'm just not ready, and that wasn't what she wanted to hear. Even though I told her when I was ready, she'd most definitely be the woman for me. She took that as meaning I didn't want to commit to her. We were both on edge and it happened fast. I'm not sure where exactly I went wrong."

"I'm the last person to give relationship advice, but when was the last time you talked to her?"

"Last week."

Oh. "Have you tried to reach out? Maybe just text her and ask if she had a good Thanksgiving?"

"I don't think she wants to talk to me right now. She's on vacation with her family, and she wanted me to go. That's how the whole marriage thing started. I didn't want to leave my gran alone. I mean she's got family, but I've never had a holiday without her, and I don't really know Eva's family.

"Eva understood about Gran. She was kind about it and even asked if Gran might want to come along. But Gran had all the family coming over, so I knew it would never happen.

"But then a few minutes later, when I said I wasn't ready to commit, she decided we'd maybe need to take a break. Those were her words. She's probably off with some surfer dude." He crossed his arms on the table and shook his head. Clueless. Poor guy.

I had to bite the inside of my lip to keep from smiling. "It sounds like, maybe, there was miscommunication. Did she hear you actually say she would be the woman you wanted to marry, if you were ready? And it isn't as if you're opposed to the idea, just not right now?"

"I think I said that, but I'm not sure."

"Maybe her feelings are hurt because she misunderstood you. Obviously, you care about her. Just reach out. Apologize—even though it's not technically your fault. Start with: I'm sorry things got out of hand the other night. I want you to know how much I care about you."

"Do you think that will work?" he asked. "I'm kind of miserable without her."

I grinned. "Maybe you should start the text or the call with that line."

He sat up straighter and blinked rapidly, as if the lightbulb finally went off. "You're good at this, Ainsley. That's some pretty good advice. I'll text her first. That way she can see what I'm saying. And I can think about what I'm writing before I do it."

"I don't think that's a bad idea." At least, I could help other people. Even if, I wasn't able to do the same for myself.

Shannon brought coffees for the three of us, along with a plate full of her pastries. "Did you guys start without me?"

Kane told her what we'd been talking about. I loved that he was open with us and truly considered us friends.

"Ains is right. You said they're on a cruise? Find out how to send her flowers. Have them waiting in her room. You'd be surprised how just doing a small thing can mean a lot to someone else."

"I should have come to you guys a week ago," he said as he picked up a bear claw. "Thank you."

"No problem," Shannon and I said at the same time.

"I have a big favor to ask. The information I'm sharing with you will be in the paper later. But I'd rather your brother not find out I was the one who told you. Deal?"

"Deal. First, was it an accident or a murder?" I asked. "I'm going to be honest, it was really hard to tell." And I hadn't bothered to look again. Once was enough with that scene. Even as my memories tried to bring it back up, the bile rose in my throat. I shoved it all down.

"Well, at first, it looked like an accident. But after a careful examination, it's just not as straightforward. That pole punctured his heart and caused instant death, and it appears someone pushed him onto that pole. It probably happened ten minutes before you guys found him. No rigor had set in, and the body hadn't been sitting for long. It's not like the television shows where I can instantly tell time of death, but it was within a twenty-minute window.

"I haven't given my final report but it looks like murder."

I leaned back and crossed my arms. "Santa choked on a candy cane and was killed by the North Pole? That's just wrong."

"Kind of an awful way for anyone to die," Shannon said, and then stuffed a large bite of an éclair in her mouth.

Kane nodded. "I don't know what he did before he was a Santa, but he had several old breaks. I would have thought maybe he was professional boxer or football player. Just about every bone in his body had been broken at some point."

Don might have an idea about that. I had to remember to ask him.

"And there was cirrhosis of the liver, though it didn't look like he'd been drinking in the last ten years. I'm waiting for the bigger tox screening to come back. They have a backlog because of the holidays and it's going to be five to seven days before I know for sure if there was something my basic tests didn't see."

"Poor guy," Shannon said, as she put her elbows on the table. "Don met him at a Santa convention but they were good friends for years. Maybe, he knows something about his past."

She was probably alluding to what Don had told us the night before without coming out and saying it. Kudos to her for being clever. I gave her a mental high five.

"I have the initial interview with Don. I think he might have been in shock because there weren't a lot of details to help with the investigation. From what was written, he and his wife had been waiting on the victim. He was supposed to meet at their home for dinner."

"That's what he said. I feel sorry for them. They'd lost touch and he'd been excited about seeing Davy again." I stared at the plate of pastries. I'd promised myself I'd stop with the sugar for a few weeks, especially after eating half a chocolate pie the night before. But maybe I'd start that tomorrow. Dealing with death was stressful.

"There was also an indication from some tissue damage in his organs and bacteria that he may have contracted a few diseases through the years. Most of them are things you might get while traveling to countries without good waste management systems and water supplies. And he was diabetic, which may have been a contributing factor. It's possible his sugars were high or low, and he stumbled. But there were handprints on his back and like I said, someone had to have pushed him back in the chair. I'll know more in a few days."

"Don did say he traveled the world. Can't you look up his medical records?" I asked.

"That's the thing," Kane said. "We can't find any. There are no dental or medical records that fit his profile. I suggested Greg talk to Don and Peggy again, but he and Lucy caught a double homicide in Warrenton. They're going to be tied up for a while."

He eyed me warily. "His friends might know if he used a different name and it's odd that he's not in the system. Not even dental records—and his teeth, except for being broken by the candy canes, had been in good shape."

Ugh. The whole crime scene was absurd.

"If you find out anything from Don and Peggy about his past, please let me know."

I pretended to act shocked and threw a hand against my chest. "Kane, are you asking me to be nosy?"

"No, Ainsley. I would never ask you to do that. Your brother would kill me. But he and Lucy are busy, and I'd really like to get his medical history as complete as possible. This guy, whoever he was, had an interesting life medically speaking. If Don, or his wife, might know another name he used, it would be helpful. I just want to make sure we're doing our due diligence. There was very little evidence at the scene other than his blood and the candy canes.

"From what the CSIs have given me so far, there were several sets of fingerprints but there's no telling when that happened."

No one had ever given me permission to investigate. This was awesome.

Kane pointed at me. "But if your brother asks, I'll deny it."

I snorted. "I know. Let me see what I can find out."

Two hours later, I walked George through the park. He'd be able to rest while I worked in the booth. As I passed by where the Santa house had been, I was surprised to see a new booth in its place—one that featured handmade chocolates.

"I need to stay away from that one," I whispered to George.

We were almost to the end where the carnival was set up. It wasn't like the cheesy ones we'd had in the past. The rides were old favorites, but had been painted to look like creatures, spiders, dragons, and even griffins were used to give the whole place a dark forest, enchanted feel.

At night, the whole place would be lit up and there were about to be some very happy kids enjoying those rides. Maybe it would make up for the lack of a Santa.

I texted my brother. *Where's Santa's house?*

It took a minute but he texted back. *County warehouse.*

I guess it wouldn't be great to leave the crime scene up where nosy people might mess up any evidence. Though, Kane had mentioned there was very little.

And it was helpful that the whole thing could be transported on a flatbed trailer. Not all crime scenes were simple to remove.

We were about to turn around, when a man I didn't

know waved at me to wait a second. He was handsome in a hipster way. He wore a beanie, dark glasses, a plaid shirt and jeans. I'm not a big fan of long beards, but his fit his face.

He half jogged up to me. "Hi," he said as he held out his hand. "I'm Rob Olen."

"Hi," I said as I shook his hand. I had no idea who he was.

"I own the carnie," he said. "You're Ainsley McGregor, right?"

Ohhhhh. I'd been talking to his manager, Rick, through email. "Yes."

"Thank you for inviting us to the festival this year. We brought some of our best rides. We have some old classics like the tilt-a-whirl, as well as some new ones. I know you guys normally use Legends. We are grateful you gave us a chance."

The Legends folks had been booked for another event. And, since I'd volunteered to run the festival committee, it had been my job to find someone new. I'd honestly just found a couple of companies online, and then checked out their reviews. These guys had a higher rating than even Legends.

"We're happy to have you," I said, as George sat down and held out his paw.

"Well, aren't you cool," the guy said as he shook George's paw. It was pretty much his only trick. And he'd known it when I rescued him. His other trick was to bark at everything that moves when he had free time outside.

"This is George Clooney."

"Man, I wished I looked that good in a Santa hat. You're

stylin', dude."

I swear George sat up straighter.

"I won't keep you. Thank you, again, for giving us a chance."

"No problem. Uh, can I ask you something?"

He eyed me warily. "Anything."

"You don't seem—you aren't—uh—like any of the other carnie owners I've met." Real. Smooth. Ains.

He chuckled. "I get that a lot. Truth is, I just started this company five years ago. I was working in corporate America and I hated my job as a programmer. I mean, I love coding. But I hate people telling me what to do.

"One day, I saw this ad for a carnival. The owner had passed away, and his family was trying to sell the rides and equipment. I put in my two weeks' notice, convinced some of my friends to do this with me, and we've been having a blast ever since. Traveling around five months out of the year, and then doing our own thing."

I admired people who took chances on their dreams—even ones they didn't know they had.

"That's awesome. Really. I quit my job teaching at a college in Chicago to open up my dream store." I pointed toward the back of my building where Bless Your Art was.

After I'd been mugged for a second time, my brother begged me to move to the small town where he'd settled. Our grandmother used to live here, and had left me her house and farm, which had stood abandoned for a few years.

I'd planned on teaching at the local university, which I still do. But then, I met several artists and crafters who lived here. It was like a mini Austin in a way. Just a lot of creative people in one spot. And the idea for Bless Your Art formed. It took me a year, and a lot of help, but we were doing okay these days.

He lifted his hand for a high five. "That's the life, right? Doing what you love."

I slapped my palm against his. "Yep. Well, I better get going. I've got to run the first shift for our booth, but if you need anything, or have any questions, let me know."

He gave me a pretend salute, and then George and I headed back toward the store.

"Who was that?" Shannon asked. She'd been walking toward us, probably trying to figure out who I was talking to. I mean, I'm not really into hipsters, but Rob was very good-looking.

"He owns the carnival."

"Really?" She almost gasped and I laughed. "He's—um, hot. Do not tell Mike I said that."

I laughed. "Your secret is safe with me." I told her what he'd said.

"That's cool. I mean who buys a carnival?"

Hot guys, apparently. "Did you see some of the other guys running the rides?" I asked. "It's like they went to a college campus and picked out the best-looking hipsters."

She laughed. "Well, the dating pool just got wider in Sweet River," she said.

"Um, says the engaged chick."

She crooked her arm in mine as George followed us back up the sidewalk. "Not for me silly, for you. Maybe you should try and make Jake jealous."

"You know I don't play games like that. Oh, I totally

forgot to tell you he stopped by this morning. Between you and him, I'll be running on adrenaline all weekend. He scared me."

"He's back? Tell me everything."

"There is nothing to tell. He just said hi, and then asked if he could hang out with George later."

"Ugh. What is wrong with that man? You're such a catch. And he's into you. Every time you're around, he can't take his eyes off you."

I was saved from answering, because Don was stringing up another row of lights above the counter on our holiday booth. "Hi," he said. Once again, sadness radiated from him. My heart tightened in my chest. I wanted to hug him and tell him it would be okay. But it never was when you lost someone close to you. I knew that from experience. "How are you?" he asked.

"Good."

George barked.

"Glad to hear it. The mayor announced they're about to open the gates, but I wanted to get another set of lights up before tonight. Peggy said she felt like we needed to make sure the place was just as bright at night."

It wasn't a bad idea. "I'm grateful for that, but we could have taken care of it."

He shook his head. "I told you I needed to get out. Your brother said they're having trouble locating next of kin. If they can't find anyone, Peg and I are going to do a memorial service for him."

I sniffed. That was just like them.

"We're happy to help any way we can," Shannon said. "I

can donate food or whatever you need."

"Thank you. Peggy's at home trying to see if she can find some letters he wrote us years ago. Maybe we can find an old address to help the police."

"Any idea what his real name might have been?"

He frowned. "I didn't know anything about that until I talked to Greg this morning. It's…just strange. He's always been Davy to me and Peggy. How did you guys know that wasn't his name?"

I didn't want him to know we'd been talking to Kane or for it to get back to my brother.

"Ainsley's been doing some research for you and found out accidentally." Shannon twisted her ponytail around her fingers. Man, she was good at this sort of thing. I'm a terrible liar. "But she hasn't found out much."

Thank goodness for my bestie.

"After I finish my shift, I'll head over and help Ms. Peggy go through the papers. I mean, unless you guys think that's too nosy."

I loved Peggy and Don like family and I refused to do anything that might hurt them or feel like I was being pushy in any way.

"Nah. She'd be grateful for the help. There are several rows of boxes piled high in the second barn. We kept saying we were going to go through them—but we just never got around to it." He stepped off his ladder, and flipped the breaker switch he'd put on the back wall.

Even though we had all kinds of sunshine, the lights still brightened everything up on the inside of the booth.

"You're amazing," I said.

He chuckled. "Thanks."

"I was wondering, do you know what sort of job Davy had before he became a Santa?" Smooth transition, Ains. I flapped my hand like a bird with a broken wing.

Shannon gave me a strange look and mouthed: *What are you doing?*

I mouthed: *I have no idea.*

"I'm just curious if maybe I could do some research and see if I could find him through his old employment records. And did he know anyone else here? You mentioned he had a friend who he was working with on his projects."

Because someone in this town might have killed him. I would not be the person to tell Don that, though. That was my brother's job. If he'd been shoved, even accidentally, it was still murder.

"He said he was a fixer. He fixed things up and worked odd jobs," Don said. "He had a nice home in Minnesota. He must have done all right for himself."

I had a feeling that Don was thinking handyman. But I watched the hotness that is Liev Schreiber in *Ray Donovan* and knew there were all different types of fixers. Not that I thought Davy was like that. But what kind of guy had best friends who didn't even know his real name?

One who was hiding from something. But what?

"Do you have that old address?"

"We gave it to your brother last night, but from what I understood this morning, he sold the home several years ago. Your brother called and asked if I maybe had another address. That's why Peggy's going through the letters."

But if he sold his home, there would be a record of that

transaction. Greg and Lucy were probably already on that, but it would be worth checking out.

"Oh, I forgot to tell you," he said. "The mayor stopped by—she was nice about it—but she was wondering if we could keep the Santa stuff going in the store. Given everything that's happened—I told her I'm happy to help out."

I put a hand on his arm. "Don, I can hire someone. Really. You don't have to do that. You just lost your friend. We can find someone else."

"Nah. It's what Davy would have wanted. Or whatever his name was. It's just odd. I mean, he's always going to be Davy to me."

I hugged him. "That's sweet. But you let me know if you change your mind and I'll talk to the mayor. I'm sure we can make other arrangements."

"Making kids happy is a joyous thing, Ainsley. I can't think of a better way to honor my friend. Don't worry," he said. "I mean it about Davy. He took the Santa thing very seriously."

Davy, who had no dental or medical records. They had national databases to track that sort of thing these days. Only someone who was truly off the grid wouldn't have any records—and he had traveled a lot. Maybe he only had his dental and medical stuff done overseas. Why else would there be no trace?

"Hey, Don, do you remember when you last saw Davy? I'm sure my brother and Lucy have a timeline, but I'm just curious."

"I guess around three forty-five. I wanted to get home to tell Peggy he was coming for dinner." I'd check with my brother but if the timing was right, that meant Don couldn't have killed him. Not that I would ever think it possible.

But as soon as my shift was over, I'd be paying Ms. Peggy a visit.

Chapter Five

After Jake stopped by the store to pick up George—no, that wasn't awkward at all—I headed out to Don and Ms. Peggy's. She was on the porch of the main house, going through what looked like a boot box full of letters.

With her curly white hair, she was the perfect Mrs. Santa, to Don's Mr. Claus. Though, she was on the thin side and when she dressed up as the big man's wife, she had to wear a lot of padding.

Today, she was as stylish as ever in her skinny jeans, oversized holiday sweater and boots. I have no idea what kind moisturizer she used, but I needed to find out. She was in her seventies, but she didn't look a day over fifty.

"How are you doing, Ms. Peggy?"

She paused rifling through the box. "I'm all right, love. How are you? Store and the festival keeping you busy?"

"Yes, ma'am. I'm very sorry for your loss. I feel bad—about everything."

She sniffed. "It still doesn't seem real to me. It's awful, but we thought he'd passed away. I'm sure Don told you, and then when he showed up in the store yesterday—Don was excited. They used to have fun together. Hurts my soul that I know my Don is suffering. He never shows it. We're at an age where we're losing a lot of our friends—but this one has hit us both hard. I think more because we thought we'd already lost him, and then just to die—violently. He didn't deserve that." She dabbed her nose with a tissue.

I reached down and patted her hand. "Can I help you with the search for the letters? Don told me you had a lot to go through."

"You're such a sweetie." She nodded.

Yep, one with an ulterior motive. But finding out more about Davy would help the police, and I'd do as much as I could.

"There's four more boxes in the truck. I did have the sense to at least date the boxes when we moved. But we piled all the letters and cards from our friends in each year's box. I have trouble getting rid of things. It's not hoarding, it's just anything with memories—I need to keep them. It's why Don built the extra barn for me."

"I think that's completely understandable." Her curly hair was piled on top of her head in a messy mop, which flopped from side to side when she moved her head.

"Thank you, dear. But after digging through all those boxes today—well, during our downtime after the holidays, I've decided to let a lot of it go. I'll keep the letters, but we have junk in there from every house we've ever lived in—it's a lot. And I don't want our kids to have to deal with it when we're gone."

My throat tightened. "Oh, don't say that." I didn't want to be in a world without these two lovely souls.

She laughed. "We aren't planning on dying anytime soon, but it was a wake-up call, this horrible thing that happened to Davy. Accidents can happen in a heartbeat and it's all over way before you might want it to be."

Ahhh. Okay. That answered one question. They had no idea it might be murder.

I picked up one of the larger boot boxes, and started pilfering through. "I'm trying to help Kane and Greg, find out something about his past. Are there any stories you remember him telling? Anything, maybe about his job before he was a Santa?"

She closed her eyes, as if she were thinking. "It's funny, we always had such a good time together, and he was an excellent listener. He'd tell us about his travels, and he had the best stories about people he'd met. I forget a lot of stuff these days, but I don't remember his discussing his personal life much. I do remember thinking, he was a very private sort of person in that way. I'd often wondered if he'd gone through a bad marriage or had worked at something he wasn't exactly proud about."

"What made you think that?"

She chewed on her lip. "It's more of a feeling. The first time he came to the house, when we were still in Minnesota, I told him he should bring his wife or girlfriend. He joked that there wasn't a woman in the world who would put up with the way he lived his life."

She sighed. "But it was the way he said it. Like, it was his punishment for maybe—I don't know—living on the edge? It was just a feeling."

Interesting.

What if he was a criminal who had been running from the law? It happened. Some fugitive would be found and his neighbors would say things like, "He was quiet and kept to himself."

Maybe, Davy had something big to hide. There was just one problem with that theory. If he was a criminal, there'd be some sort of record of an investigation. Kane had mentioned they were without any good leads in that direction.

We were silent, only the birds chirping on the big live oak in the front yard. I flipped through letters. I stopped when one was postmarked from New Zealand. There was no return address, but the postmark was definitely from there.

"Do you mind if I peek inside to see who wrote this?" It was odd going through someone else's correspondence, especially with them sitting right there. But incredibly interesting at the same time.

"Not at all, dear. That's why you're here. Don and I have nothing to hide. And we're lucky that we've had many wonderful friends through the years. I'm happy to share them with you."

I carefully opened the letter and skipped down to the bottom; it wasn't from Davy. But it was from one of their friends, and a highly entertaining letter about trees bigger than houses she'd seen in New Zealand. I kept going through the pile and was almost to the bottom an hour later, when a postmark from Thailand caught my eye.

I opened it up and several photographs fell out. They were from different sites from Bangkok to the Phi Phi islands. I consider myself fairly good at geography—even though I get lost every time I go somewhere new, but even I hadn't heard of a lot of these places. A few of them were scenery, but two of them had a picture of an older, slightly plump gentleman. He wore sunglasses so it was hard to tell if it was Davy.

I read to the bottom and it was signed by Davy. He told them about the places he'd been in the country. But it was the last few lines that caught my attention.

"This trip has been tougher than most physically. Maybe it's the heat—I hate to admit it but I'm getting old. I think my days traveling the world have come to an end. I'm ready to put down some roots back home and be with family. Hope to see you both soon!"

Did he have family? "I think I found something." I handed her the letter. She read it and then handed it back to me.

"I don't remember him ever talking about family. That's interesting. He called his friends his family, though. The family that you make, he used to say. He was proud that he had people to hang out with all over the world. And he'd taken to calling me Sis.

"I'm old and my mind is not what it used to be. And we were all big drinkers back in the day. Lord only knows the conversations I've forgotten. But he never really had a family of his own. Always called himself a lone wolf and he liked it that way."

"Do you mind if I take this to my brother? Also, since he was in Thailand, maybe we can check the passport number for information." I had no idea how that worked or even if the police had a database that could pick someone out by a picture. But I did have the date he was there, so that was something.

"I'm going to get some iced tea. Would you like some?"

"Yes, ma'am."

She opened the door of the farmhouse, and then turned back to me. "Oh, I meant to ask, where's George? You know he's always welcome here."

"Thank you. He adores you guys. He's playing football with Jake."

She chuckled, as if that made all the sense in the world. It probably did. George Clooney was a celebrity in town. People usually said hi to him, before they noticed me. He really was a great dog.

I picked up another box, just as a car rolled up. It was a light blue VW bug and very recognizable.

What are they doing here?

Ms. Peggy must have heard them, because the screen door banged against the wood frame.

"You need to come with us," Ms. Helen said. Today she wore a pink tracksuit that said, *I'm Juicy*. Ms. Erma was dressed in all black, which was her normal uniform since her husband died more than twenty years ago. The two women were some of the busiest busybodies in the county. There was not a shred of gossip these two couldn't find or share.

"Why?" Ms. Peggy asked, and she didn't bother to hide her exasperation. While the other two women lived to gossip, Ms. Peggy was all about just letting people be.

"They've arrested Don!" Ms. Helen screeched.

What did my brother do now?

Chapter Six

THE POLICE STATION was a madhouse, as in there were at least twenty people crowding the small lobby, screaming at Kevin, who ran the front desk. The poor guy was not equipped for this and had a deer-in-the-headlights face. I was about to say something when Ms. Peggy put two fingers to her mouth and gave a shrill whistle.

"Stop yelling at that poor boy," she said, as she put her hands on her hips. "What has gotten into you people? I'm here to see my husband and I would appreciate it if we could have some decorum. My nerves are already shot. We lost a dear friend, and I heard my husband was arrested. If any of you think your thing is more important, raise your hand."

Everyone stared at their shoes, including me. She was pretty soft spoken most of the time. I imagine they were just as surprised as I was.

The door to the station opened and I turned to find my brother with the same deer-in-the-headlights face Kevin had.

He held up a hand. "If you're here about the Christmas thief, we're looking into it. If you're here about Don, he was not arrested. He's here to help us figure something out."

Christmas thief? *I wonder what that's about.*

"If you'd like to file a complaint or report stolen items, please line up in an orderly fashion and Kevin will help you out. If you've come to complain about Mr. Clark, you can leave. As I said, he is *helping* with the investigation."

While I seldom listened to my brother, he did have an authoritative way about him. Ms. Helen and several others exited past my brother. Everyone else moved into a line against the wall.

"Mrs. Clark and Ainsley, please come with me." I was surprised he included me. He's usually in more of a *stop butting into police business* mood.

We followed Greg to his office, where Lucy and Don chatted amiably. They were smiling, which was always a good sign.

"I'm sorry," she said to Greg when he walked in. I'd never seen her apologize for anything or appear contrite.

"Well, you did walk Santa Claus away from his place of business through the busy streets. At least you weren't wearing your Santa suit. We might have had a full-on riot." He smiled at Don, who chuckled.

"We walked *together*—there's a big difference. I forget sometimes how small towns tend to see things." Lucy folded her hands in her lap.

"Lucy, you met Mrs. Clark, Don's wife, last night."

"You can call me, Peggy," she said. They shook hands. Then she hugged her husband. "You causing problems, old man?"

He hugged her back. "Always."

I adored these two people. They had one of those relationships that others aspired to have. There was such a deep love there. And they were kind and funny. In my head, and I know this is ridiculous, they were the real Mr. and Mrs.

Claus.

"Since we can't find next of kin, I asked Mr. Clark to help us identify the body," Lucy said.

Poor Don. I was thinking that a lot lately. I prayed he'd only had to see his face. Even that couldn't have been easy.

"And we need to delve deeper into the victim's history," Lucy continued. "We're trying to find out who he really was. His fingerprints are impossible to trace because at some point, years ago, from what Kane said, his fingertips were burned. We're grateful for anything you can tell us."

Lucy stood, and offered her chair to Peggy, who took it. She seemed to notice me for the first time, but didn't say anything. I moved to the back wall, and sat on the edge of the credenza. Lucy leaned on the frame of the office doorway.

"Do you know if he had any family?" Greg asked. "We're sorry we had to ask you to identify him, but we couldn't find anyone else."

"It's okay," Don said, but his voice was low and it was more than obvious seeing his friend like that had not been a pleasant experience. "He was never close to anyone in his family," he said. "At least, as far as I know. He always called me the brother he never had, and Peg the sister. I'm not sure if he has or had family somewhere, but he never talked about anyone specifically. I always had the feeling he was a loner."

Peggy rubbed her temple. "And the fingerprints—he's had those scars on his hands since we met him. I think he told us how he got them, but for the life of me I can't remember the story."

"A fire when he was a kid," Don added. "They were

burning brush on some land his grandfather had. I can't remember exactly what happened, just that he had his hands bandaged for almost a year. Back then, they didn't have the kind of treatments they have today. By the time we met him around twenty-five years ago, the scarring was mostly white and hard to see."

"Oh, that's right. He was always accident prone. I remember him saying that. And a daredevil. He was kind of proud that he'd broken nearly every bone in his body before he was thirty."

Well, that maybe explained what Kane had seen with the bones.

"Do you have any idea why he might have changed his name?" Greg asked.

"There are no records for him anywhere. According to our databases, he never existed," Lucy interjected.

"I'm as shocked as you." Don frowned. "In all of the years I've known him, I never once thought he wasn't Davy Santos. He was a great friend and whip smart. It was clear he'd been to college and had some sort of professional degree. Numbers came easily for him. He helped me invest in some stocks, most of which paid for our place here. But he knew a lot about many different things. Said he'd picked it up on his travels, working different jobs."

"And he was smooth, in a charming way," Peggy added. "He could talk anyone into anything. That's how Don and I ended up skydiving for the first and last time. We did a lot of that sort of adventure thing with Davy. His only real faults were that he was an adrenaline junkie, and couldn't sit still for long. But he was always there when we needed him. At least, up until a couple of years ago, when he seemed to just disappear."

And then he turned up here, of all places. I had an idea my brother and Lucy were thinking the same thing. Why was he in the middle of Nowhere, Texas? Don't get me wrong, I love our town. And we have great tourism these days. But it's not exactly a place we'd expect to be a hot spot for a guy who traveled the world.

And how odd was it that there was no record of the guy ever existing?

I pulled the letters and photos out of my bag.

"What's that?" Greg asked.

"I helped Ms. Peggy go through some boxes and found some letters. He did talk about putting down roots and reconnecting. There may be someone out there who is missing him." I handed the letters to Greg.

My brother stared at me for a minute. And it dawned on me that I'd been caught butting in. But he just shook his head. "He might mean reconnecting with people who are like family, such as the Clarks."

He had a point. They'd just said pretty much the same thing.

"There are stamps and dates—I was wondering if there was a way to maybe check passports, like find his picture and see if he was using an alias."

I expected my brother to comment that I'd been watching one too many thrillers.

Greg opened the letter and read it, and then glanced through the photos. "We found his passport in his belongings in his car. He used the same alias for everything, including selling his house."

That answered that question, and the guy was able to get his hands on a fake passport. I'm sure that isn't as easy as it looks in the movies.

What kind of people did that? People who were hiding and had the connections. And, um…spies. No way I'd say that here, as my brother would laugh me out of the office.

That old show *In Plain Sight* whooshed through my brain. Maybe because I'd been bingeing it, along with *Vera* most nights, until I passed out. I also have a girl crush on Mary McCormack, who stars in that series.

"Um. What if he was in witness protection? I mean, not as Davy but as someone else. Ms. Peggy said he was a good listener, but never really talked about his personal life other than his travels. Or is that too *In Plain Sight* or *Vera*?"

"Who is Vera?" Lucy asked.

"A great British detective on television," Greg said. "And you may be on to something. I don't know about witness protection but you're right about leaving out parts of his life."

It was all I could do not to laugh about the *Vera* comment. I'd forced him to watch one episode when I'd been recovering from being poisoned, and then we ended up bingeing a whole season over a weekend.

"I know you don't have the equipment here, but what if you sent his picture to someone who could do facial recognition, like the FBI?" I asked.

Did I mention I watch a lot of crime shows? But I'd helped with enough real-life cases to understand it was seldom simple to solve a crime, especially murder.

"We've been focused more on who would want to kill him," Lucy said.

Don and Peggy gasped. Uh. Oh. No one had bothered to tell them that Davy had been murdered.

"What?" Don was furious. "Who would want to hurt Davy?"

Lucy glanced at me with surprise in her eyes. Yes, I knew it was a murder, but for once I'd kept my mouth shut.

She seemed surprised.

"I'm sorry," she said. That was the second time she'd apologized and it might have been a record. "I didn't realize you hadn't been told."

"He was the most likable guy in the world," Don said. "Always smiling and would never hurt anyone. I can't imagine why someone would want to kill him. That doesn't make any sense. I thought it was an accident."

Greg glared at Lucy. For once, I was glad I wasn't at the other end of that stare. "Kane ruled it a suspicious death this morning," Greg said. "There is evidence of foul play."

Ms. Peggy sniffed, and Don handed her a handkerchief from his pocket. "My husband is right. No one would think about hurting Davy. He was just the best."

The Clarks almost had me convinced. And from the few minutes I'd spent with Davy, he'd been quite nice. But he'd lived a long life, and there was no telling what might be in his past. It might have even happened before he ever met the Clarks.

Whoever killed him might have accidentally shoved him from behind and he stumbled onto the pole. But then, why not confess right away?

The look on his face as he sat in that chair had been one of surprise.

Kane said he'd died instantly upon impact.

Crud. He was right. It was murder. I don't know why I had some hope that it was a terrible accident.

Because the idea of having a killer running around makes you nervous.

Chills went down my spine. There had been a lot of people around the park that day. The suspect list could be endless.

Except, most people knew their killers.

"It's a lot to ask when you're grieving, but if you remember anything about his past—it doesn't matter how small, please call me or Lucy. I want to thank you both for coming in." Greg stood. "We appreciate it."

"You'll let us know when you find something, right?" Ms. Peggy asked. "I'm fairly certain that we are the closest thing to family he had. We want to do right by him, and we'll hold a small memorial service—that is if no one claims the body."

"Of course, we will let you know as soon as Kane gets back to us with his final report. But it might be a week or more. Just please understand that."

The couple nodded in unison.

"Lucy, why don't you walk them out. I need to talk to Ains."

The investigator didn't appear happy about that, but she gave the couple a quick nod and followed them out the door.

"Why wouldn't she just call Don and ask him to come in, rather than parading him through town? Didn't you learn your lesson last time?"

Kevin, who worked the front desk, had been sent to escort Mrs. Whedon, my favorite octogenarian, to the station when she was finished with church the last time George found a dead body.

Only, Kevin was overzealous, and interrupted the sermon and mirandized the poor old woman in front of all her friends. It had not been pretty.

"Lucy was just doing her job. Though, a call might have been better. I was helping out with a case in Warrenton, and I wasn't here."

I smirked, but what I really wanted to do was ask him about the case he'd been working on. He had that weary look about him, like he'd seen too much of the dark side, and I just didn't have the heart to bring it up.

"I have a strange feeling," I said.

"Have you eaten yet?" he asked, as he sat back at his desk. I took one of the chairs in front of it. "Or maybe it's that you eat pie for breakfast. Your sugars might be crashing."

I rolled my eyes. I do that a lot when my brother is around. "It's not my blood sugar. It's about Davy. Maybe I'm reaching, but this guy went to a lot of trouble to hide his identity. And all his travel—it just makes me think he had something big to hide. Like maybe he has a criminal past or he's on the run from some very bad people."

Greg tapped a finger on the desk. "I've been thinking the same thing, but then how would they find him here? It's not like Sweet River is a bevy of criminal activity."

"Right. But it has to be someone from out of town.

Think about it. We have people from all over the place with booths at the festival. We're like the new Round Top, this time of year. Maybe they recognized him? If he was diabetic, he could have been unsteady?"

Oh. Darn you, Ainsley. Keep your mouth shut.

My brother smirked. "Someone has been talking to Kane."

"You don't know that. Don or Peggy might have known."

He stared up at the ceiling. "Your idea to see if the FBI can help identify him is a good one. I'm going to call Cal in Dallas and see what he can do. If this guy was ever a person of interest, there should be a record somewhere. And since there aren't any court papers showing a name change, that may be our only hope, unless a family member comes forward."

They'd gone to college together and Cal was good about getting Greg what he needed.

"I hope he can help."

"I have a job for you as well."

Wait. My brother was asking for my help?

The apocalypse is nigh.

"Two things… We have someone who is stealing Christmas decorations from homes and store displays. I need you to keep an eye out."

"The Christmas thief?"

He nodded. "Probably some kids pulling pranks, but you know how this town feels about its decorations. Just let me know if you see or hear anything."

"What have they taken so far?"

He flipped open a file on his desk. "A wreath, a small animatronic Santa and a few dozen strings of lights."

"That's crazy. Who would do that?"

"I have no idea, which is why I need your help. The town leaders are up in arms, even though the grand total of the stolen goods is less than a hundred dollars.

"And then the other thing, and I want you to be careful with this one—as head of the festival committee, I was wondering if you could stop by the vendor booths. Maybe introduce yourself, and see if you hear anything about Davy. Don't get too nosy asking questions. Just chat with them, and then let me know if you see or hear anything suspicious. Do not get into trouble."

"Gregory McGregor, are you asking me to snoop? I'm pretty sure hell just froze over."

He snickered. "You're going to do it anyway. Just be careful. Don't ask too many questions. As much as I hate to admit it, you do have sense for finding killers. Unfortunately, not always before they find you. It's about being careful."

"Got it."

I had permission to do my favorite thing.

Would it be as much fun?

Yep. I'm embarrassed to say I hadn't been that excited in a very long time.

There were many people working the festival and one of them might be a killer.

Chapter Seven

After leaving the station, I'd planned on going home and taking a hot bath. These early mornings were killing me the last few days. But I decided to hit up at least a few booths, to cross them off my list. I stopped by Bless Your Art to pick up my clipboard and the list of businesses selling wares and food.

My phone buzzed.

Where are you? Shannon texted.

In the store.

Come to the booth.

I locked my purse in my office, and then headed out the back door.

A few steps later, I was at the booth, which was crowded on the side with the shop's wares.

Yay for us!

There were a few people lined up on the food and drink side where Shannon poured coffee. Ben, who worked at her shop, took the payments and provided the pastries.

She waved. "I'll be right there." After hanging her apron on the side wall, she headed my way.

"The weather turned chilly and everyone and their brother decided they needed a hot drink." She laughed. "And Maria and her daughter Carrie have had to refill your side at least three times while I've been here."

"That's good news."

She pulled me toward the shop. "What happened at the station with your brother?"

I didn't bother asking how she knew about that. Word traveled fast around here.

I gave her the rundown and that I'd been given permission to ask around.

"I can't believe he's letting you ask questions. Usually, it's the opposite."

"I think he and Lucy are really busy with another case in Warrenton, and he's desperate for help. And his other choice was Kevin—"

She giggled. "Poor Kevin. He'd probably end up arresting everyone."

"True. Also, I think my brother knows I'd be asking around about Davy anyway. This way he can control it to some degree, and keep me out of trouble."

"You'd think he'd understand by now that you're a magnet for trouble."

She wasn't wrong.

"I was actually talking to some of the booth owners, who stopped by to get coffee. A lot of them travel to the same events."

"Oh? Did you find out anything?" One of the reasons her coffee shop was so successful was that Shannon had a way of making everyone feel like she found them the most interesting person in the world when she was talking to them.

"They are here for the next two weeks. But in April

they'll be at Round Top. And then a lot of them also do Brimfield, Massachusetts, in September, which the lady at the candied ornament booth told me. Also, her chocolate orange ornament is the best piece of chocolate I've had in a long time. Melt in your mouth kind of good."

The side of my mouth quirked upward. Shannon sometimes took a minute to get to the point.

"Anyhoo…the thing is, a lot of them knew the guy who died. They were asking me questions and trying to see if I'd heard what happened. I played dumb. But they all said the same thing, it was sad, because he was the nicest guy they'd ever met. Like, went out of his way to be kind and helped take care of people. I heard story, after story, of folks he'd lent a hand in one way or another."

That's what Don and Peggy kept saying.

If he was such a nice guy, why did someone kill him?

"But there's one lady, Caroline. She has the booth with all the unusual lamps. Don't buy the Man on the Moon one. You might get that one for Christmas."

I chuckled. "Um okay." She was talking so fast I had a tough time keeping up.

"Right. I think she and the Santa guy maybe had something, something going on. She seems to be super sad, as in started crying when I was talking to her about what inspired her to create such amazing work. When I tried to find out how she knew him, she clammed up."

She took a deep breath. "Sorry, I'm talking ninety miles an hour. I promised Mike we could go to dinner tonight and I need to rush home and change. Otherwise, I'd come with you." She frowned and then dug through her tote, coming up with her keys.

I glanced out over the long line of booths. There was no way I could talk to everyone tonight. It would be silly to try. But at least I had a lead. "That's okay. I appreciate you telling me. I may just go look for some new lamps."

My brother had been right. As the festival chair, it would be good for me to get to know the vendors we had here. And it didn't hurt to do a bit of checking on backgrounds. I planned to keep notes on anyone who seemed interesting.

"Okay. I'll see you later. Text me if you find out anything."

"I will."

After she left, I headed down the pathway to the woman she'd been talking about. Everything closed up at eight, and it was seven thirty. I didn't have a lot of time. Hopefully, this first stop would be a good one.

At first, I thought no one was in there. And then a woman with long black hair, who was dressed in leggings and a giant sweater, popped up from behind the counter, yelping.

"I didn't know anyone was here," she said. "Sorry about that. Can I help you?" Petite didn't begin to describe how tiny she was. She probably wasn't even five foot. She held a glass lamp that was in the shape of a Santa.

"I wanted to introduce myself. I'm Ainsley McGregor the festival chairperson." I held out my hand. She put the lamp down and shook hands. "We wanted to say how much we appreciate you coming here. You guys have a lot of choices this time of year and we are grateful you chose Sweet River."

"Oh, that's nice. I'm not sure anyone who ran a fair has

ever greeted me like that. Thank you. I'm Caroline Mendoza and this is my first time to Texas. Beats Minnesota where I used to live. I love this weather."

That's where Don and Peggy had met Davy.

"I used to live in Chicago. I totally relate. It's one of the reasons I moved here." It snowed maybe once every few years in Sweet River, though I hadn't seen any yet.

"I moved to Lubbock about two years ago," she said. "My bones just couldn't take another winter."

That's when the Clarks had lost touch with Davy.

"I'm curious, do you make all of these?" I nodded toward her lamps. The glass and metal work was intricate and delicate.

She waved a hand over her wares. "I do. Some of them are blown glass, others are glass pieces I pull together to create a light sculpture. My dad was a welder, and my ex a glass blower. I learned a great deal from both of them."

There was another man on the moon lamp, and it was stunning. I had no idea how she was able to string all the glass and wire together to create such wonder.

"You're very talented. Before you leave town, you should come up to my shop. I'd love to sell your lamps at Bless Your Art. If, that's something you might be interested in doing."

"Oh, I was there earlier. That's yours? It's amazing. I've been around to a lot of places, but I've never seen anything like it. In a way, it reminds me of the bazaars in Morocco, but air-conditioned, and not as loud and jam-packed. You've organized it well."

I chuckled. "Trust me, I have a lot of support. Do you do a lot of traveling around the world?"

Her smile faded. "I did with my boyfriend Davy. He knew all the interesting places. That's where I was able to find inspiration for several of these pieces. But I don't know about the future."

She sniffed, and put a tissue to her eyes.

"Oh? I'm sorry if I upset you."

"No. No. I can't even process that he's gone. He's the one who convinced me to come here because he had friends in town he wanted to see. And I feel guilty because if I'd been on time, maybe—sorry."

Shannon was right. Bingo.

"If you'd been on time?" I asked softly.

"Maybe he'd still be alive. I'm always running late, which he liked to make fun of. But I wanted to get set up at the campground. I'd brought a few of the boxes and then left. I told him I'd be back in an hour but—when I came back, he was gone."

Well, there's another alibi. Maybe. She could be lying. And if she was his girlfriend, that would most likely make her suspect number one.

"I'm sorry for your loss. You seem to have been very close."

She sniffled again and her lips thinned into a straight line, as if she were barely keeping it together.

Way to go, Ains. Make the poor woman cry.

"Oh. My. I've put my foot in my big mouth."

She cleared her throat. "It's okay. It's just that he treated me like a queen. We had a blast traveling together. He showed me the world and was one of the best friends I'd ever had. I loved him. I really did."

There was a great chance she might know Davy better than anyone. Tears trickled down her face. I had questions but I forced myself to stop.

"Well, if you need anything, just let me know. Or even you just want to talk about your friend, I'm here. Those folks he wanted to visit here are great friends of mine. You should meet them. I bet you all would have wonderful stories to share.

"And when you're ready, I'd love to chat about selling your stuff in the store."

She dabbed her nose with a tissue. "Aren't you adorable. Thanks. I will. And please, tell his friends I'd love to meet them."

"I'll do that."

I waved goodbye, and then texted Greg. Was she having an affair with Davy? They'd traveled the world together. She'd called him boyfriend the first time and friend the second. I'd picked up on that.

I'd give Caroline some time, and then I'd try to talk to her again.

My phone dinged and I glanced down, assuming it was Greg following up. But it wasn't. It was a picture of Jake without his shirt, standing with George, who had a football in his mouth and looked like the happiest dog in the world. I swallowed hard. Those abs of Jake's were something else.

I started laughing. Not at the abs, but at the fact they were covered head to toe in mud.

Good news is we won. Bad news: we got dirty. George is home with me. He's much cleaner now.

He sent another picture of George chasing chickens.

Be there soon, I texted back.

George would like a hamburger. And his friend Jake would like a cheeseburger with fries.

Well, maybe things weren't as bad as I thought between Jake and me. Shannon had said that I didn't try to contact him either. Communication was a two-way street.

If he was asking me to pick up food—I don't know what it meant but at least we were texting.

He sent another pic of George passed out on the back porch.

I snorted—just as I slammed into someone hard. My phone went flying and my breath left my chest.

Large hands steadied me and kept me from falling on the path.

"Oh, darn. Sorry, Ainsley. I was looking at my phone and didn't see you." It was the handsome carnival owner.

"Me too," I wheezed.

"Are you okay?" He let go of my arms and looked me over.

I nodded. "I'm good." I took a deep breath. "I should have been watching where I was going."

"Same," he said. "I know this is random, but why don't you come to dinner with me and my friends?"

"What?"

"You know, it's the meal that comes after lunch. I feel bad for nearly knocking you over. Let me make it up to you."

I glanced over his shoulder, trying to spot his friends. "You don't have to do that."

He frowned and looked behind him and then belly-laughed. "I just realized I probably came off as a total creeper. Let me try again. My friends and I would like you to have dinner with us. Not just because I nearly knocked you over, just to thank you for letting us be here."

"I'm fine." I waved him away. He was just being nice.

"We would like to hang out with you. I told the gang about you and they want to meet you. Anika is fascinated by your store. She already thinks you're brilliant."

"Plans. I mean, I have them. Tonight." *Use your words, Ainsley.*

He chuckled. "Okay, how about tomorrow night? The gang and I were going to check out Dooley's Diner. Did you know that guy was on the Food Network?"

"I did. And trust me, you will love his dishes. Let me check the schedule for tomorrow—not sure when I volunteered to work."

"We'll probably do it after we close tomorrow. Maybe around seven-ish, since we close at six?" Before I could say no, he did a fake salute and then went on his way.

He didn't seem like a guy who took no for an answer. It didn't matter, I needed to talk to the carnie friends anyway. It'd give me a chance to see if any of them knew Davy.

And he probably only asked me out because he and his team wanted to come back next year. Not that he was using me, but they wanted to stay on friendly terms.

The thing was, I already had every intention of asking them back. Their setup was unusually creative for a carnival, and it added a lot to our festival.

After stopping for burgers at the Dairy Queen, I drove out to Jake's. His farm was next to mine but not too close.

We could see each other's lights at night but that was about it.

I pulled up his long drive and gathered his bag of food. I left two burgers in my passenger seat for George.

I stopped, and gathered my thoughts. Everything had been awkward earlier. I valued Jake as a friend; he'd been there for me when I'd been in the hospital, and after. I wouldn't let anything drive a wedge between us.

Jake's farmhouse was built in the same style as mine, with intricate mill work. That's where the similarities ended. His house was painted a deep navy with white trim. It was gorgeous. Mine was a soft yellow. It was kind of crazy how much of a difference paint made but I was a fan of both houses.

And his was a working farm and he had four times as many acres as I did. There were horses, chickens, a couple of cows, a barn cat named Killer Kitty, who was about as mean a feline as I'd ever seen. Jake joked that she'd grown up on the mean streets of Sweet River. He'd found her near an abandoned building a few years ago.

She was not a big fan of George or me. In fact, I was certain she hated me more than she did George.

Stop stalling. Just drop off the food. Get George and go home to your lonely little house. At least, I had a date the next night. Okay, it was a group of people. But still, an invite, nonetheless.

I forced myself to open the car door, praying that tonight wouldn't be as awkward as it was this morning. As I approached the front porch, a light flickered on above the door.

Here goes nothing.

George woofed from behind the door. At least, someone was happy to see me. *I will not make this weird with Jake. I will not make this weird with Jake.*

He opened the door.

George went straight for the bag. "And here I thought you were happy to see me. You just want food." I held the bag up high and handed it to Jake.

"In his defense, he played really hard today. I bet he sleeps well tonight."

"How did you guys get so muddy?"

He chuckled. "We were at the park over by the lake. The ball went out of bounds and straight into the water. Before I could stop him, George jumped in and got it. But the banks were super slippery from the rain last week, and he couldn't get traction. The team worked together to pull him out. It was like the ten Stooges. He's not light. I wish we had it on video—we could win one of those contests on television."

I laughed, and my nerves fled. "Well, I'm glad you at least had fun."

"We did." With the hand that wasn't holding the bag, he patted George's head. "He's funny and he plays seriously at the same time. It's almost like he understands what's really going on."

George, my traitorous dog, leaned into Jake. He did that all the time with me. But it's a Great Dane thing. I read it in a book somewhere.

"Come on, George. Let's get you home." I turned toward my SUV.

"Wait, you're not going to eat here?" Jake asked. "I thought maybe we could catch up."

I faced him again. I'd survived the last few minutes without making a fool out of myself but it had been a long day. "I can't tonight. I have some things to do." Like wash my hair, put on my favorite pajamas and watch *Vera*.

A woman had to have her priorities straight.

"How about tomorrow night?"

I almost made another excuse, even though I'm a terrible liar, and then I remembered I had a real one. "I have a date tomorrow night."

Liar. I don't like playing games but it bugged me that Jake thought I had nothing to do.

I mean, he'd be right most nights, but he didn't need to know that.

He flinched as if I'd punched him in the face.

What was that about?

"Who with?"

Why did he care?

It didn't sound cool to say a guy who owns a carnival. "Just someone I met today. Super nice guy." And since I had no intention of talking about my dating life with Jake, I ushered George into the back seat.

"Bye," I said out my driver's window.

And then I headed home. If I really was going out tomorrow, I had to do things like find something to wear. Even though Rob had made it clear it was a group thing.

There was a hundred percent chance I was not going to fit into any of my good jeans. Not after the last few days of Thanksgiving leftovers.

"George, I might need to go shopping in the morning. Oh. Darn. It's Sunday. Even with the festival, the stores, including mine, would be closed until noon. It was South Texas after all.

"Scratch that. I'll be shopping in my closet. At least, I have those cute tops I bought at Junk Gypsy." Shannon and I went to Round Top at least once a month to see what they had new there. I'd bought a flouncy red blouse that hid a multitude of sins.

A vehicle was in my driveway. "Who is that?" It was a new black SUV but I'd never seen it before. Someone moved on my porch. I turned on the light over my front door with the app on my phone. Ever since I'd been nearly killed twice at home, my brother had insisted on installing all of the bells and whistles a security system could offer.

The figure on the porch moved into the light, as if sensing my hesitation.

"Ugh." What is she doing here?

Chapter Eight

I DROVE AROUND the SUV and parked under the carport on the side of my house. I had a garage, but it was full of inventory at the moment. We'd run out of room in my barn.

"Hey," I said as George and I climbed the porch.

"Sorry to show up like this," Lucy said. She was in jeans and a sweater. I wasn't sure I'd ever seen her out of her suit that she wore like armor.

What is she doing at my house—this late at night? I mean, it was barely eight, but the town usually rolled up the streets at six. And only a dispatcher and a couple of officers worked at the station after seven. If anything went wrong, my brother was usually the one they called.

"Is Greg okay?" I'd just talked to him before I left the park about what I'd learned.

"He's fine. He asked me to come out and talk to you about the woman you interviewed."

"Oh?" I mean, it's not like I had anything super special to tell. It could have waited until the next day. "You didn't have to come all the way out here for that." After unlocking the door, I motioned her to go inside.

"I won't take much of your time," she said stiffly.

"It's not that. I just feel like you wasted a trip." I turned on the lights, and then headed to the kitchen. "Let me get

George fed, and I'll tell you what I know."

After pouring kibble into his bowl, I put one of the hamburgers on top. He ate it in one gulp. Lucy chuckled behind me.

"I guess he likes burgers."

"He pretty much likes everything except for radishes and pickles. And he'll even eat pickles if they're on a burger or hotdog." I washed my hands and then stuck the other burger in the fridge for a treat later. If he ate too much junk at once, it wouldn't be pleasant. Great Danes have sensitive stomachs.

"I was going to heat up leftovers for me. Would you like something?"

She shook her head. "I don't want to trouble you."

"It's no trouble. I have a ton of food from Thanksgiving. You'll be saving me from myself."

"Okay. Thanks."

"Have a seat and I'll heat us up some plates."

"Your house suits you," she said, as she turned around, seemingly taking everything in. Law enforcement is like that. Always aware of their surroundings.

"I'll take that as a compliment," I said. I loved the homey atmosphere I'd created here. I'd blended pieces from my modern Chicago loft, with French country antiques my grandmother had left here when she died. It all seemed to work and I adored the relaxed feel of it. Nothing was too precious.

"You should. Are you sure I can't help you?"

She was being so friendly and it made me even more suspicious about her motives. "Nah. I've got it. Do you like cheesy green beans?" It was a family favorite but it wasn't for everyone.

"It has cheese, I'm in."

I laughed. "I feel the same way. Also sweet potato casserole, turkey and cranberry sauce."

"It all sounds great." She sat down. "I worked on Thanksgiving, and I missed out on the food. But you didn't have to go to all this trouble."

"I have to feed myself. It's just as easy to feed two people and I am getting tired of leftovers."

George had finished his meal by the time I'd heated everything up in the microwave. I let him outside for his nightly run, washed my hands, and then took everything to the table.

We ate for a few minutes. I was hungry, especially since I'd missed lunch. That rarely happened.

"You asked about the woman I talked to. I told Greg that she and Davy were close. She was so sad, it was heartbreaking. She shared a bit but not a lot."

After pulling out a notebook, she wrote some things down. "What exactly did she say?"

"They'd traveled together all over the world. I didn't want to pry too much because she was obviously grieving. But I got the feeling they were serious. It's odd though. At first, she called him her boyfriend, but later on, she said friend."

Lucy pursed her lips together and then frowned.

"What? Did I say something wrong?"

After laying her pen down, she crossed her arms. "No. It's just—"

"Look, I know you like to keep things close to the vest.

And this town is rife with gossips. But I'm not one of them. I can keep a secret."

Her eyebrow went up. "Until the suspects land on the murder board for your *book club*." She did finger quotes around book club. She had a point. It wasn't a huge group and the board allowed me to keep things straight in my head. Almost all the murder crime shows used them—including *Vera*.

"Well, as far as I know, we don't have any suspects yet. Right?" I stuffed some turkey in my mouth to keep from saying too much. "What do you think happened, exactly? You were able to examine the scene right after the…incident."

Her pen stopped on the page, as if she were thinking about what I said. "You've spoken with Greg and probably Kane, right?"

I didn't want to get either of them in trouble. My brother had brought me into this for once, but I didn't think it was a good idea for her to know that Kane had been talking to me as well.

"It's possible."

She grunted. "Then you know there might have been an altercation and the victim fell on the pole. There was a pool of blood where the pole had been, and death was instant. Kane hasn't been able to determine if the candy canes were in his mouth when he fell. To me, it seems like they would have fallen out so they must have been placed there afterward, and he was pushed back into the chair."

I sighed as the visions of that scene came flooding back. I'd seen everything and my mind held on to details like that, making it feel as if I were back in the moment.

I rubbed my temples. "You can let my brother know that we've suspended the book club through the holidays because everyone is busy. There will be no whiteboard. You don't have to worry about that." I would, however, keep everything in a notebook and on my computer. Just so I didn't forget any details.

She took a bite of turkey and then put her fork down. "I'll share information with you, if you promise to do the same." She didn't appear to be super happy about that. It must have taken her a lot to come out here.

"Deal."

"Like I mentioned, Kane is certain there was foul play. Once the victim was impaled, it would have been impossible for him to stand back up and sit down without assistance."

I'd gathered that when we spoke at the coffee shop. Then there were the candy canes in his mouth. Was that a signature from the killer? Albeit a really strange one?

The Candy Cane Killer. I could see it in the papers now.

"Okay. Do you have any suspects?"

"Our main one was Mr. Clark at first, but he has an alibi. And after speaking with him earlier, I can't see him as the person we're looking for."

That's why she'd gone to the shop and walked him over. It was an intimidation tactic, which cops often used to make the suspect nervous. I was ready to say something, and she must have realized. She held up a hand. "I know. I know. My working assumption, though I usually try not to assume anything, is it was an argument with someone. He'd been pushed from behind and accidentally fell on the pole.

"The candy canes are confusing, though. The victim might have been yelling for help and the murderer, who probably panicked, stuffed the candy in his mouth to keep him quiet. It's an assumption, but from what I saw at the scene, it fits.

"But Kane believes, from the way the candy was lodged in the victim's throat, that they were there when he fell on the pole. The physics of the whole thing are odd though. Usually, Kane says, the force of something like the North Pole going through a stomach would shove enough air through that the victim would have coughed them out."

"Why would you even think it was Don?"

"An hour before the murder, he'd been seen working on the Santa house. There were several witnesses. At the time, he was the only person, other than his wife, who had a connection to the victim. They have a history together. And though they were friends, friends sometimes argue. You know as well as I do that murder victims usually know their killers."

My body tensed. She had better not be going down that path. "Don was excited that Davy was in town. And he and Peggy are mourning their friend's death. He's also the kindest man you'll ever meet."

"Ainsley, everyone is capable of murder in the right circumstances. Like I said, Mr. Clark has an alibi for the time of the murder. He's no longer a suspect. But I would appreciate you talking to him again. There may be something from the past that might assist us in figuring out who this guy really is."

"Is that why you came over?"

She smiled and it changed her face. "No. I came to apologize. I've been reading the reports of the investigations you've been a part of, and you have a natural ability to get people to talk to you."

I had no idea why that was. It was as if there was something about me that made them feel comfortable about spilling their life story.

"Your brother wanted to talk to you face-to-face, but he was called away tonight. He sent me to make sure you were okay. And to ferret out any more information you might have learned."

I hoped Greg was safe and okay. I tried not to think about the dangers of his occupation but it was tough sometimes. It was one of those things I was good at shoving down emotionally. Otherwise, I'd do nothing but worry about him. We gave each other a tough time but he was the only family I had left.

"We talked about it tonight and most people aren't crazy about speaking to cops. Especially, people who travel around these festivals. Greg talked to you earlier, but you need to understand we do not want you to put yourself in danger for any reason. Your brother asked me to stress that. You don't need to dig too deep or make people suspicious."

My throat constricted and my stomach tightened. "Okay. But I'd already talked to him and promised I'd be careful." The words came out harsher than I'd meant.

But it was odd he'd sent her.

"Yes, but I think he had second thoughts after you sent him the news about Caroline Mendoza. You seemed to home in on her so quickly. You do have a knack for this. We've spent the last twenty-four hours trying to find someone close to him. And you did in a matter of minutes."

My head popped back in surprise and this time it was my eyebrow that went up.

Did she just give me a compliment?

She cleared her throat and leaned forward. "There's something I had to explain to you. I think we got off on the wrong foot the first time we met. When I'm on the job—I—I'm a woman. And it's still an old boys' club, especially where we are. You're the sheriff's sister and I didn't want to look like I was taking it easy on you. I may have been tougher on you than was necessary."

I'd been sipping tea and almost choked. I grabbed my napkin to wipe the dribble from my chin.

"When it comes to being bullied—are you talking about my brother? I'll kill him for you." I held up my hands in surrender. "Wait, I shouldn't say things like that to you."

She laughed loud. I wanted to tell her she should do it more often and a lot of people would want to talk to her.

"No. He's fair and honest, and treats me like an equal. But the rest of the guys—they aren't super crazy I made lead investigator over them. Some of them have been trying to move up for years. I work for the county, which is why I'm not always here. And I have a position where I'm involved with different departments, most of which are made up of men. It's…not always fun."

"I'm sure it's not like it is on television shows and movies where the women detectives are always celebrated."

"No, it isn't." She uncrossed her arms. "This job means constantly watching my back and every word that comes out of my mouth. I'm not alone. A lot of women, especially law enforcement in Texas, are still dealing with all this. I could go to a bigger city, but I'm not sure it'd be any easier. And Greg's a great boss and a friend. Did he tell you I've been staying with him? As a roommate, of course."

Uh? "No. I didn't know."

She steepled her fingers. "I've just gone through a really bad breakup and I needed a place to stay. People talk, especially in this town. But just in case you stopped by—I may be there awhile. We are friends—that's all. Besides, I don't think I'll ever date again."

"I totally get that. I'm glad you're here to hang with him and that you feel comfortable enough to do that. I'll deny it until my dying day, but he is a good guy."

She grinned. "He is. I've been thinking about reapplying to Quantico. I had to drop out of the program when my mom got sick. But I also like what I'm doing here. Your brother is giving me time to figure it all out and I'll be forever grateful to him."

"I guess he's okay," I joked.

That good ole boy network was something I had to overcome when I was trying to get my permits for the building. Someone else had wanted to buy the property and they tried to make it tough at first.

Until I told Greg what was going on. I did it out of frustration but the next day the clerk called me back with the permits.

I don't like using anyone that way, but I'd probably still be waiting for the permits if it hadn't been for my brother.

It was odd that she seemed to want me to like her. "Do

you like my brother?"

Her eyes went wide. "He's one of the best cops I've ever met," she said. Then she looked down at her fork as if it were the most interesting utensil in the world. "And like I said, I'm not interested in dating anytime soon."

But she didn't say, no.

Stop nosing around. There's no reason to put her on the spot. But it did make a sister wonder.

"Do you want pie? I have chocolate cream and pecan left."

She chuckled. "I'm good, but thank you. I should probably get going. I've got an early shift tomorrow. But if you could keep talking to the people at the festival, Greg and I would appreciate it. We'll pick up the woman you were speaking to tonight—for a longer chat. Thanks for the lead. Hopefully, she knows who our victim really was."

I had my doubts about that. Caroline didn't seem much like a murderer but it was best not to assume. She had an alibi, but that would need to be checked.

I needed to remember that lesson about assuming. Believing people were nice and incapable of murder almost got me killed a few months ago.

In the heat of the moment, there was no telling what people might do.

I'd be smarter about that this time.

Chapter Nine

THE NEXT MORNING, I slept in and felt better than I had in the last week. The store was usually closed on Sunday, but the festival would open up around noon. They wanted to give people time to get home from church. While our town was fairly progressive, church was a thing. I went every once in a while—okay, I went on holidays because I liked the music—but I loved that sense of community.

By the time I made it to my parking space behind the shop, the grounds were abuzz with activity. It was seventy degrees and it looked like the whole town, and a fair number of tourists, were doing early holiday shopping.

I let George out of the back seat. "We're going to be around a lot of people today. You need to be on your best behavior."

I swear if he had an eyebrow it would have been raised.

"I know you'll be good, I'm just setting the expectations."

He grumbled.

I attached his red leash that matched his collar and plopped on the Santa hat. Once again, he stood taller like it was a badge of honor. "Let's go, handsome."

After making sure Maria and Carrie were set for their shift at the booth, we sauntered down the grounds.

First stop was a booth that sold intricate wooden ornaments and figurines. It was a sight right out of a German Christmas market.

The man behind the counter had an I-teach-at-Harvard outfit with his tweed jacket, bow tie and starched white shirt. He couldn't have been more than forty and it was odd that he was dressed formally for the festival.

"I haven't seen these in a long time," I said as I checked out the three-tiered pyramid-thingy. I had no idea what they were called. Each one was intricately hand-carved and there was a windmill on top. These varied in size from small desktop ones, to ones at least three foot tall. "You put candles in and the heat makes the tops turn, right?"

"Yes," he said. "We call them pyramids. My partner and I make them." He had an English accent, and reminded me of Daniel Kaluuya, who played W'Kabi in *Black Panther*. I'm embarrassed to say how many times I've watched that superhero movie. But I genuinely loved it.

"I wish I could buy them all—they're wonderful." I held out my hand. "I'm Ainsley McGregor. I own Bless Your Art at the top of the hill, and I'm the chairperson of the festival. I wanted to thank you for coming out. Quality craftsmen, like you, just make this place even more special."

He gave me a wide grin. "Thank you. It's been very busy, and if that first day is any indication, it might be one of the more profitable Christmas festivals we've done." His language was as formal as his attire. "You and the committee who put this together did a bloody wonderful job. These things aren't always organized so well."

"I appreciate that. Do you and your partner do many of

these events?"

"We have a shop in Austin, but we travel for a month in the summer and in December. My partner and I are gypsies of sorts, and we love glamping."

Glamping was fancy camping. I hadn't tried it. Mainly because nature didn't always like me. I was prone to mosquito bites and wasps liked me a little too much.

"We have employees, and friends, who run the shop for us during the busy season, so we can travel around. It sounds contradictory, but it works for us. We like meeting new people, and neither of us is particularly happy being stuck in one place too long."

"They have chocolate-dipped Twinkies." A man with red curly hair stepped behind the counter. "We'll have to run an extra five miles tomorrow but it's worth it."

They laughed.

"This is Ms. McGregor, the one who runs all of this," the man with the bow tie said. His partner wore a polo and khaki shorts. Less formal, but still better dressed than most of the booth owners, including me.

"Ainsley, please." I held out my hand to shake the red-headed man's. "And I have a ton of support to make this happen."

"I'm Armand," the first gentleman I'd met said, "and this is my husband, Justin."

Figured, the handsome black man was married to Prince Harry. Wait, was he still a prince? I could never keep the royal drama straight.

"You are a gorgeous couple. And your work is magnificent. I never use that word. But your creativity is astounding."

"Thanks," Justin said. "May I ask you a question?"

I guess as the chairperson it was my job to listen. "Sure. Do you need anything?"

The two men looked at each other.

"What?"

Armand leaned down on the counter. "What happened to Mr. Davy?" he whispered.

Well, this might be easier than I thought.

"Can I ask why you would think I'd know the answer to that?"

The two men smiled.

"You're in charge of the festival and we figured you'd hear the latest. And you have the same last name as the sheriff, who talked to us earlier to ask if we'd seen anything. Is he your husband?" Justin asked.

"You guys *are* clever. He's my brother. And, as far as the suspicious death, it's a matter of public record. The medical examiner is still running tests but it wasn't an accident."

They glanced at each other again and frowned.

"How well did you know him? Do you think there's any reason why someone might want to hurt him?"

"We didn't know him very well," Justin said. "He worked an event we did last year. The German market in Arlington, Texas. He was a Santa there and he had a booth with the most incredible toys. We bought a few to sell at the shop."

There was a long pause.

"Why do I get the feeling you do know something?"

"Mr. Davy was beloved by everyone—except a few of the

husbands."

"Husbands?"

"I've never seen anything like it," Justin said. "The women were all over him. That first day, we saw him with the lady who has the lamps. And then two hours later, he was coming out of Mary Beth's trailer and he was adjusting the waistband of his pants." He angled his head to the right.

The booth next to them was filled with various kinds of quilted holiday blankets. The buxom blonde was dressed from head to toe in hot pink. And her booth was directly across from the woman who made the lamps.

Could it have been jealousy? What if Caroline found out about his trysts with the hot-pink lady? Sex was one of the biggest reasons people killed one another. Sex and money.

"You think maybe one found out about the other and there was a fight?" It would fit the crime scene.

Justin gave a slight headshake. "It isn't just those two. He had a way with the ladies. We are the last people to judge. And I have no idea if he was actually sleeping with them all, but he was a flirt. I do remember a guy yelling at him when we were in Arlington. It sounded like he was pretty angry that Davy had spent time with his wife."

I wonder how Caroline feels about him getting around? She seemed pretty serious about him and if he'd been cheating on her...

Well, that was motive for murder.

Several customers walked up to the booth. And Armand gave me a quick wave.

"It was great to meet you. I'd love to hear more about your shop in Austin. Maybe tomorrow we could grab some coffee?" I liked these guys, and I hoped maybe they'd let us sell a few of their things in the shop. The more variety and unique gifts we had, the better we did.

Nothing wrong with asking a few questions and increasing revenue at the same time.

"Sounds like a plan," Justin said.

At least, I had a lead. My hands shook at the prospect of talking to the woman in hot pink they'd pointed out.

She wasn't just a lead. She could just as well have been the person who murdered Santa. Jealousy and sex were a dangerous combo. That is, if she'd known about Caroline and the other women.

George had fallen asleep on the ground and it took some time to get him up and moving.

"A couple more stops, and then we'll visit the guy with the dog treats."

At the word *treats*, he cocked his head and his tail wagged.

"That's a handsome dog," the woman they'd called Mary Beth said. She opened the top of the counter and walked around. "Is it okay to pet him? I have a thing for Great Danes. If I didn't travel so much, I'd have one."

Well, she was quite friendly for a murderer.

Never assume anything. I had to keep reminding myself of that.

"He'll love it. I'm Ainsley McGregor. I—"

"Oh, you have that adorable shop up the hill," she said. Then she gave George a big hug. "Don told me about it. He's a friend of—I mean, was a friend of Davy's."

"I do own the shop, and thank you. Were you and Davy

close?"

She faced me. "I'm going to miss that old fart. Davy, not Don. I just met Don." She rubbed the bridge of her nose with her fingers. "I still can't believe he's gone. Never had a man who could make me laugh like he did. Like a hard belly laugh. He had the best stories."

What is it about me? People tell me stuff without me even trying too hard. Shannon said it was my kind smile, but I wasn't sure about that.

"I'm sorry for your loss."

She hugged me. Right there in the middle of the festival. I wasn't in the habit of hugging strangers, but I hugged her back. Then she sighed.

"Were you guys dating?" It was the nicest way I could think to ask the burning question.

"Oh, Lord no. Women loved him but as a friend. He was a huge flirt. I never want to get married again. I haven't exactly been lucky in that department."

Interesting. I definitely needed to check out her past.

People aren't always what they seem. I'd learned that lesson the hard way, a couple of times.

"Would you like a cup of tea? I have my special blend. And I have some cookies for your friend here."

"Oh, I wouldn't want to keep you."

She waved a hand. "I'd love the company, if you've got the time. Please." She looked so hopeful.

There was no graceful way to turn her down. "Sure."

We sat down on the stools she had set up behind the counter. She gave George a couple of shortbread cookies. A few minutes later, she set a lovely china cup and saucer in front of me. George was happy to be in the shade, and was already snoring.

Have I mentioned he sleeps about twenty-two hours a day?

A woman walked up and asked about the dragonfly quilt. It was the only one without a Christmas theme. I'd been eyeing it the last few minutes. Six hundred dollars later, the woman walked away looking very happy.

The quilt was worth three times that.

Mary Beth sat down on the stool next to me. "Drink up, honey." Then she gently clicked her teacup against mine.

I took a small sip of tea. *Please don't be poisoned.* "Oh, my. That's the best tea I've ever had."

She chuckled. "It's good for the soul. It's the mix of cardamom, cinnamon, and orange. I love it around the holidays but I drink it whenever I need a lift."

I could sniff it all day. It evoked memories from long ago of the holidays at my grandmother's home, which was now mine.

"Is it hard being on the road all the time?"

"Nah. Most of us are gypsies at heart. Not actual gypsies, mind you. But sitting home waiting to die is not how I want to live my life. Out here I get to meet interesting people like you." She held up her cup and drank a big gulp.

"Do you know many of the vendors who are here?"

"A few. A lot of us who live in Texas end up at the same events. I go to few outside the state, but I like staying closer to home. Y'all have done a great job of getting folks from all over. Pretty soon, you'll be giving Round Top a run for their money."

I leaned forward. "I can't take credit. It's been growing for years before I got here. Do you know any of the Texas regulars?"

"Yes. Quite of few of them. I love Armand and Justin. Those boys are a hoot. And that English accent. I don't care if he's gay, still melts this old girl's heart."

I chuckled.

"You said Mr. Davy was a flirt. I'm curious what you mean by that?"

"Oh, honey. Ya know, old people have sex, right?"

I choked on the tea.

She laughed, loud. "When you get to be my age, ya take what you can get. I mean, not in a sad, pathetic way. Like I said, I don't want to get married again. And I enjoy male company, as much as the next girl."

I really did not want to hear about a seventy-year-old woman's sex life.

Not that I had one. But still. There were some things I didn't need to know.

"Do you think maybe one of his other—friends was jealous?"

"You mean, Caroline? Nah. She spent more time with him than anyone else. They have the travel bug, like a lot of us. But Davy is friends with everyone he meets, and there's nothing she could do about that.

"For her, I think it was more about the friendship. They had a lot of fun together but it's never been serious. At least, from what she's said to me. I only met them last year at another festival. He worked with me on contracts when we were in Round Top in September. Like, he understood all that crazy legal rigmarole and the financial side of things from my last husband's trust."

Wait, if there was a trust, did that mean her last husband had money? Then why would she be working a quilt stand?

I really needed to check her out, but I didn't want to look rude.

"I thought he just played Santa?"

"Oh, Lord, no. He was a jack of all trades. He usually has a booth with stuff he's picked up from around the world and amazing toys that he makes. Stuff you just don't see everywhere.

"We called him the toymaker. Though, he couldn't work a booth while playing Santa in December, which is why he didn't have one set up here. He had a thing about money. Caroline and I offered to run it for him, or let him put stuff in our booths, but he wasn't having it. Also, he refused to hire anyone. It was the only thing he'd get testy about—money, that is.

"When I met him last year, he was playing Santa. The kids just loved him—I swear it was in his soul. Never met a man who was always in such a good mood. Never had a sad day. But he told me last year that every day of his life was a blessing. And that he wanted to help as many people find joy as he could."

"Did you see him the day he died?"

She pursed her lips. "Yep, he visited the campground where a lot of us are set up. I told him he could stay with me—but he had a place. Said he liked his privacy. I'll be honest, I'm kind of surprised he didn't bunk with Caroline."

Maybe that's when Armand and Justin had seen him

coming out of her trailer.

I needed to check with Greg to see if they found anything wherever he'd been staying. Or maybe Lucy. She might be interested to know that he had more than one lover.

Ugh. I still had him as Santa in my mind. It was freaking me out.

"Was there anyone else he might have been seeing? Maybe a reason someone might want him dead?"

She gasped, and George's head popped up.

"Wait. Are you saying he was murdered? Oh. Lord. There's a murderer around here." She said it loudly, and people passing by turned and stared.

"Uh. Sorry." I explained what Kane had said. "I was just curious. I can be nosy sometimes. I didn't mean to upset you."

She held her hand on her chest. "That just scares the pants off of me. I'm a woman traveling alone and even though we all sort of look out for one another, you can't be too careful these days. But no, I can't imagine anyone wanting to hurt him. I'm sure your doctor guy is wrong. It was definitely an accident."

She seemed sure about that.

"Did you happen to see him again here?"

She shook her head. "No. I didn't see him that afternoon. I was too busy getting things ready."

For someone so well liked, Davy had died in a terrible way. Lucy was right about the candy canes. It was just too crazy. It's not like the guy would have done that to himself. But no one needed to know that right now. If they found out, they might not talk as easily.

I had seventy-one more booths to go. "Thanks for the tea, but I need to go."

"Do you mind if I come up to the store sometime this week? I know you have quilters already, but maybe we could chat?"

"Of course, I'm working Tuesday—come on over then."

"Thanks again."

I tugged George up again, he wasn't happy with me. "Tell you what, dude, we'll go to the dog bakery guy next."

He perked up again.

"You take care, honey." She patted George on the head.

I made good on my promise, and then we hit up about twenty more booths. None of them knew Davy.

Then a sliver of the conversation with Mary Beth stuck in my brain. The contracts and the money. Everyone had said he was easygoing and smart. He might have been a lawyer, but with the exception of my uncle, I'd never known a happy lawyer. Or maybe a finance guy. She said he was eccentric when it came to money.

He could be a secret criminal mastermind.

Nothing surprised me anymore, but I had a hard time believing Don and Peggy would be bamboozled by someone like that.

What if back in the day he had been, though? Maybe he worked for bad people.

Not every lawyer works with gangsters, Ainsley.

That was the problem with getting most of my detective skills from television shows and books.

But I'd learned to trust my instincts over the last year.

We found a picnic table to sit at. George ate another one

of his treats and tried to look sad for the kids walking by. A few asked if they could pet him, and pretty soon George was in kid heaven. They were oohing and aahing over him.

I used my other hand to look up Mary Beth.

Nothing came up at first, and then I found her.

Oh. My.

Mary Beth had outlived four husbands, three of whom died under suspicious circumstances—even though they were all later found to have died of natural causes. There were several articles. She'd been cleared on every case. But that was a lot of old dead men. And there were poisons that often made it look like natural causes.

Another thing in the stories was that she always seemed to be out of town when they died. I'd learned on an earlier investigation that alibis often had holes.

I glanced up to see Mary Beth chatting with Caroline. It didn't look like they were upset. But when Mary Beth turned around to head back to her booth, she frowned.

What was that about?

"George, let's go look at lamps."

"Thank you for stopping by," Caroline said to a customer, as she handed them a bag with a bow on it.

"Even your packaging is pretty," I said.

She smiled. "Oh. It's you. Thank you."

"I admire how you've been able to keep working after everything that has happened."

She stopped and then frowned. "What do you mean?" Her eyes narrowed.

Walking on tricky ground here.

"I'm sure since you guys were close, you've heard that

there were suspicious circumstances. Do you know who might want to hurt Davy?"

If there is such a thing as an evil eye, I was most definitely getting one.

Before she could answer, I pointed to a lamp that was made to look like the Eiffel Tower. "Oh, I need that for my guest room. Even though I'm not big on theme rooms, I ended up putting a lot of the stuff I'd gathered on my travels in there."

Nothing like a distraction to throw her off guard. There was no way she'd be strong enough to shove Davy, though—unless he wasn't feeling well.

"Do you want me to wrap it for you?"

I fake chuckled. "No. You don't have to put it in a bag even. I can just carry it to my car."

She shook her head. "I don't mind wrapping it up to protect it. The glass is delicate."

"I appreciate it. Sorry for being nosy. Did you get to meet Don and Peggy yet? They loved Davy. I feel like the faster the police find out what really happened, the sooner everyone will be able to rest easy."

"It makes no sense. No one would want to hurt him. He's was the kindest man I ever met. I'm really not sure how I'm going to live without him." She sighed.

"I've done it again. Put my foot in my mouth. I really didn't mean to upset you."

"It's okay, hon. It's actually nice to talk about it. I can't believe the police think anyone would hurt him. I thought for sure it was an accident."

I stuffed my hands in my pockets. "How long had you

guys been dating?"

She stared down at her feet for a minute, as if she were preparing what she wanted to say. Interesting.

"Oh, I would never call it that. Davy didn't like the term or anything else that smelled of commitment. And I was okay with that. I've been around awhile and have no desire to take care of a man again. We just liked hanging out and we were good travel partners. I'm sure you've probably heard some of the rumors about him and women, but he was all talk. A huge flirt yes, but all talk."

That was quite a different story than I'd been hearing. Armand and Justin had seen him coming out of Mary Beth's adjusting his pants.

Was Caroline trying to throw suspicion away from herself?

Jealousy was an evil partner in crime.

"I've been all over the world with him. Everyone who met him loved him. He was such a giving soul and I think people can feel that. I will miss that the most—the kindness."

Her lips thinned and she swallowed hard, as if she were trying to keep from crying.

I'm a terrible person.

"Let me know if there's anything I can do."

"Thank you. You asked why I keep working? Because it's taking my mind off of things. I'd be sitting alone in my trailer not sure what to do next and probably crying all day. He was the best friend I ever had." Her voice wobbled at the end and it nearly did me in. "I'm just gonna miss the heck out of him."

There was no way this woman killed Davy, accidental or otherwise. "Thank you for this." I nodded at the wrapped lamp. "If you need to talk to someone, I'd love to hear about Davy. He was such a wonderful friend to Don and Peggy. They had the best stories about him."

"Oh, I'd love that. We did have some fun. It might be good to talk about the positive things."

"Take care." I took the bag from her and waved goodbye.

But when I turned around to encourage George to start walking again, Mary Beth was staring at me with a strange look on her face. There was no way she could have heard what we'd been talking about.

I remembered the articles about her husbands' deaths and I shivered.

I texted Greg and Lucy.

I'd see if they'd meant what they said about sharing information.

Because I had a doozy of a tale for them.

Chapter Ten

"WAIT, THIS GUY was a seventy-year-old gigolo?" Greg asked. We were all in his office, with George finally getting his afternoon snooze in on the dog bed Greg kept for him.

"No. That's not what I'm saying. I'm not sure he was anything more than a flirt and the women definitely didn't pay for it," I said.

"Highest cases of STDs are people in nursing homes," Lucy added. "Don't be old-fashioned."

"I think I'm more grossed out that Santa was getting around." Greg smirked and then tossed his pen on the desk. "What is it with people these days? It's all kinds of wrong."

"Ageist," I said. "Even though the women seem to be cool about it, I don't think you should rule out a crime of passion. Caroline seemed pretty in love with him to me, even though she swears they were just best friends. And Mary Beth, I don't know. She's a sweet lady and she loved George. I can't see her as a murderer." I'd never thought about how tough this was. My brother and Lucy probably had to deal with seemingly nice people who did awful things all the time.

"Ains," Greg said. "We'll do a more thorough background check on her and make sure she has a solid alibi.

Anyone could have pushed him on that pole."

I shivered at the mention of the word "pole." I could not get that image out of my head.

"You said there was something else," Lucy said, and then slurped her Coke. I was kind of jealous. She and Greg had been eating Dairy Queen when I walked in. Fries felt like a really good idea after all of this and George and I had done a lot of walking today.

"Everyone keeps talking about how smart he was. At first, he seemed like this happy-go-lucky guy who traveled the world and liked to play Santa. But Don, Peggy, and these women all talked about how brilliant he was. And he assisted them with contracts. So what if he was a lawyer? Maybe one who worked with some not-so-nice people and had to change his name."

"Ains—"

I held up a hand. "I know, I watch too much television. But he had enough money to make his way around the world a couple of times. It's just something to think about. Did you guys get a hit on the facial recognition?"

Lucy sighed. "It's the weekend. They won't even put him through the system until tomorrow."

"Lazy," I said. "You guys work twenty-four seven."

"Right?" Greg said. "Listen, we have to get over to Warrenton on a case. Oh, wait. Don't forget to keep an eye out for the Christmas thief. He hit a couple of the stalls at the festival last night. Nothing worth much, but we don't want the town or the festival to get a bad reputation."

I'd totally forgotten about that. "You have cameras set up all over the festival, can't somebody go through it?"

"Yes. Thanks for volunteering."

Lucy chuckled.

"Me?"

"Well, I'm shorthanded at the moment. It's either Kevin or you."

Kevin is a nice guy and pretty decent at answering the phone. But following through on tasks is not one of his strong suits.

"Fine." I pretended to be the martyr. But it was exciting. That Greg, after all his yelling at me, was willing to let me do this—wait a minute.

"Are you giving me this menial task of looking through videos so I'll stay out of trouble?"

"I'll get you set up."

I walked right into that.

Three hours later, I'd gone through the last couple of days of footage. I backed it up to the day of the murder. Santa walked into his house, and then a short while later, Don came out, he turned and waved. He had a big grin on his face, and was not the murderer. Maybe Lucy hadn't seen this tape, or she wouldn't have thought for a second Don could kill anyone.

A short time later, someone walked in but I couldn't make out if it was a man or a woman. They wore a hoodie, and dark jeans and it was as if he or she knew there were cameras. The wacky thing was—they never came out.

I watched it again, carefully. Nope. No one came out. Shannon and I walked toward the building. "Dear Lord, George, is my butt really that big?"

My dog sighed.

"I'm going to assume that means yes."

I didn't really care that much about my size, but it might have been time to add less pie and more walking to my schedule.

I rewound the tape and watched it again. No one came out. What happened to the guy in the hoodie?

There had to be a back entrance, but I didn't remember seeing it. I'd been more focused on poor Santa, and Greg would have never allowed us to go back in. I mean, it's not like I would have wanted to. Just thinking about it brought that coppery scent of blood to my nose.

"I wonder if Greg will let me take a look?" He'd said the house had been taken to the county warehouse but I had no idea where that was.

I fast-forwarded and caught another shadow.

"It's a kid." He had a string of Christmas lights in his hands and then he was out of the frame. It could have been a girl. The child wore a ball cap, jeans and a hoodie, but the shadow was much shorter than the guy I'd seen go into Santa's house.

If it was just a kid pulling pranks—

I continued to watch the video. Earlier in the morning, Mary Beth and Caroline were talking. They were animated but not in a way that showed they were arguing. And then they hugged.

"I don't know about you, but I need food and maybe a nap."

George grumbled. Probably, because he was already taking a nap.

We walked back to my car, which was still behind the

shop. I popped the lock and ushered George into the back seat.

"Hey, Ainsley?"

I turned to find the carnival owner, Rob, running toward me. "You still up for dinner at Dooley's?"

I'd forgotten. Yesterday felt like a hundred years ago. "Sure. Let me see if I can find a dog-sitter for George. Dooley won't let him stay outside the diner anymore. He's a big fan of the food and whines too loud. It's pretty much the only time he misbehaves in public. The food is that good."

He laughed.

I was about to call Jake—but no. I couldn't. Not after last night. It was too much.

I texted Shannon. She agreed immediately.

"I need to run George out to my friend's house. I'll meet you over there around seven?"

"Sounds good. The crew is excited to meet you."

I guess I had a group date.

Chapter Eleven

DOOLEY'S DINER WAS one of the few places in Sweet River that stayed open past six, even on Sundays. Except tonight. The sign on the door said he had a family emergency.

I hope everything is okay.

Footsteps pounded on the sidewalk. A guy in a hoodie, much like the one I'd seen in the video. I was just about to scream, when hoodie dude said, "Ainsley. I found you."

It was Rob.

I'm glad I didn't scream. That would be a terrible way to begin a date.

"When I didn't see you here at seven, I thought you might be looking for me. I've been running all over the grounds to see you if might be there." He put his hands on his knees as he tried to catch his breath. "I might need to up my cardio."

We laughed.

"After I took George to my friend's house, I ran home to take a shower." I was fifteen minutes late, which was unusual for me, but after being outside all day—I'd needed to freshen up.

"No problem—except a change of venue," he said. "Come with me, we've gone with plan B."

Was he the guy in the video I'd seen earlier? Lots of men and women wore hoodies, especially this time of year.

Stop being suspicious of everyone.

"What's plan B?"

"Me and the gang put together a camp fire where we've parked our trailers. It's at the other end of the park."

"Oh. Do you mind if we drive over? I'm parked behind my shop. That way I don't have to walk through the park in the dark to go home."

"Sure. Though, I'd be happy to walk you back."

"I appreciate that but this is easier." I'd worn my boots with the three-inch heels. They looked pretty, but no way did I want to walk a mile in them. They were already pinching my toes. But they looked great with my dark jeans and red top. Rob wore dark jeans, and his hoodie was open to reveal a ZZ Top vintage T-shirt. It worked on him.

We made it back to the shop, and as we climbed in my SUV, I caught a whiff of a clean pine scent. I didn't know anything about Rob, but I did like the way he smelled. I pulled around on to Main Street, and then took a right at the stop sign. They were set up in the parking lot across from the park.

It was a new lot the city had put in last summer, since our many holiday events were pulling in more and more tourists and parking had become a problem.

"You guys aren't out at the campground with the others?" I asked as I pulled up. They'd taken over the far corner of the lot. There was a long tractor trailer, which probably transported the rides, as well as four huge flatbeds. There were a couple of RVs centered around a campfire in the middle of the big trucks.

"Nah. For security purposes, we have to stay near the carnival. Two of us are always on watch to make sure kids, and sometimes adults, don't try to take free rides. You'd be surprised how many people try to sue you when they've been stupid."

"Really?"

"Yeah. We had a situation in Arlington where a couple of teens tried to start up the spider, the one with the twirling cars and eight arms. You need a key, but they were smart and jerry-rigged it. It started up and conked one of them in the head. The parents tried to sue, but the kid only had a concussion and technically, because it was after hours, it was considered breaking and entering. The judge tossed the case. But it taught us a lesson."

I chuckled. "People are dumb."

"Right? Come on, I want to introduce you to the gang."

He motioned to a lawn chair and I sat down. There were four other people sitting around the fire, which was nice and warm. It was only sixty, but there was enough of a nip in the air that the fire was great.

"That's Anika." He pointed to a woman in her early thirties. She had an Afro that was to die for, and wore a colorful blanket around her shoulders. "She's our money person. In her former life, she was a forensic accountant."

Anika gave me a bright smile and waved. "This—" she swirled her hand around "—is much more fun than being stuck in an office with fluorescent lighting all day long."

"I can imagine."

"That's Rick." He pointed to a young black guy with

Harry Potter glasses. "He's the one you were talking to through emails and he books all of our tours. He used to be a mechanical engineer for Bell, but now he keeps our rides safe and running smoothly."

Rick didn't look old enough to do any of those things. His emails had been so formal and professional, I thought he was an old guy.

"Hey." He waved. "It's nice to meet you, Ainsley. I need to run and check on dinner." He popped up, and did a slow jog to one of the RVs.

"He's also an amazing cook," Anika said. And the way her eyes followed him, I wondered if they might be dating. "He has a big treat for us tonight."

"Scott and Brewer are on watch. Scott does a lot of our PR and social media, and runs a couple of the rides. Brewer is a reformed finance lawyer and a jack of all trades. We haven't found anything he can't do. But he's also responsible for making sure we have all the proper permits before we get where we're going."

"It's nice to meet you. I've heard a lot about the rides. Everyone is loving the carnival."

"We're just grateful Legends wasn't able to come, and you invited us," Anika said. "This is our biggest event yet."

"Can I say something, and you guys won't take offense?"
They frowned.
"No. No. Nothing bad. I just feel like you guys are the most un-carnie people I've ever met. Usually—well, they are pretty rough. And they don't look like they hang out in hipster bars."

They laughed, hard.

"It's our version of running away with the circus," Anika said. "And so far it's worked out pretty well for of us. We haven't killed each other yet—but I think it's because we're all so different and everyone brings a different talent to the group."

"You aren't wrong," Rob said, and then scooted his chair closer to mine. Probably so he didn't have to yell over the fire, which was crackling pretty hard. "I've known all these guys for a while. Most of us met in college, except for Rick. He went to Harvard, but he did his doctorate at SMU, and my office was across the street. We met at Trinity Hall Pub one night during a soccer game. And we've been best mates since."

If they went to SMU that meant they had wealthy families and could probably afford to run off to play carnival. Or, they'd had steep school loans.

"It's cool that you guys were friends who went into this together. And brave."

I started my business on my own, but if it weren't for the people who sold their wares in my store—we wouldn't have been such a success over the past year. And they had all become my friends—from the octogenarian Mrs. Whedon, to Maria, and Don. We'd become a close-knit group. I wasn't just invested in them business-wise. I wanted success for them in all aspects of their lives.

"Yeah," Anika said. "We all sat down and set up some ground rules. We're also taking off in January to give us time apart. But we've found our groove and it's great that we all love what we're doing. Keeps people happy when it doesn't feel like work."

"Dinner's ready," Rick said from the doorway of the camper.

"Let me get that," Rob offered, and jumped up from his chair by the fire.

They brought out trays for each of us. Shrimp and grits, which happens to be one of my favorite meals, an apple salad, and iced tea. I took my tray and sat it in my lap.

"Oh, I should have asked if you wanted something other than iced tea," Rob said. "We have beer, wine and juices."

"This is great," I said picking up the glass of tea. "And fancier food than we would have had at Dooley's. Though, when he's back you guys have to try his chicken-fried chicken. I don't know what he uses in his batter, but it's addicting as crack. I mean, not that I've ever tried crack."

Nice, Ains. Way to make friends.

Anika howled. "She's funny. I like her."

Whew. My sense of humor doesn't always translate to others.

The conversation lulled while we ate. They hadn't lied about Rick's skills as a chef. This was the sort of thing you found in Austin or Dallas. And definitely not something you'd expect would be made in an RV.

"This is incredible," I said as I scooped up the last of the grits. "I may stop by for dinner every night."

"You're always welcome," Rob said. "Can I ask you something?"

"Yes." I was about to stand up and take my tray to the camper, when Rick jumped up and took it for me. "I can wash the dishes," I said.

"No way," Rick said. "It's Anika's turn tonight."

"He's right," she said, gathering up the trays. "Our little group works because there's an equal division of labor, and we all take turns with the menial tasks. Except for cooking; Rick does most of that."

"Thanks." I turned to face Rob. "What was it you wanted to ask me?"

"I saw you going from booth to booth today, talking to everyone. Is it about Davy?"

I glanced around the campfire, as the others leaned in.

"I'm not a police officer, if that's what you're asking. I'm an English teacher who runs Bless Your Art and the chairperson for the festival. I was making the rounds and saying hello to everyone."

That was sort of true. And why did this group care? I had the feeling this invitation was more than them thanking me.

"It's just that we heard you were asking a lot of questions," Rob said. "We were wondering if you knew anything about what happened to Davy. We all really liked him and we heard it wasn't an accident."

And there it was. Is that why he'd really asked me out? To find out what I knew about the murder?

"My friend and I are the ones who found the body. It was disturbing." Still true. "He was a dear friend of a friend, as well, but if you know anything specific, I could pass it on to my brother. The sheriff."

Anika had been walking toward the RV, when she turned to look at me.

Why would it matter to them? Rob admitted he didn't know Davy that well.

But was he the one going into the Santa house? The outfit was the same.

"We were just curious if he was murdered," Anika said bluntly. "There are all kinds of rumors circulating and we were worried about the safety of some of our friends. There are a lot of women who travel alone to these things."

I chewed on my lip. I liked this group of people but they were strangers. There was no way I'd be sharing information. I also didn't want to fuel any rumors that might be going around.

But Greg had said a part of the story would be in the paper. "Sweet River is one of the safest places I've ever lived. They are waiting for more information to come in, but the ME has ruled it a suspicious death."

There was a collective gasp.

"So, definitely not an accident?" Rob asked. "And why do they think it was suspicious?"

Red flags went off in my head. They were definitely trying to find out what the police knew. I think maybe it wasn't just about Davy or the safety of the women working as vendors. What if one of them was in the Santa house?

What if it was Rob, and that's why he was being so flirty and nice?

It was time to do some digging into this carnival of theirs.

Did any of them have a criminal past?

"Give her a break," Anika said. "And stop trying to be a television detective. You have to forgive Rob. He's a big fan of that old show *Lie to Me*, and is into micro-expressions, which we all know is not an exact science. He even does it before people get on rides, and he's constantly trying to analyze us, which is extremely annoying."

Everyone laughed, including Rob, defusing the tension.

"I'm not sure what to think," I said honestly. "Everyone seemed to adore him."

They all nodded.

"Happiest guy ever," Rob said.

"You didn't notice anything different when you saw him the other day? You said you guys had met last holiday season."

He shook his head. "Nah. Still happy Davy. Never saw him without a smile on his face."

"And good with the kids," Anika said. "If I didn't know better, I'd swear he was the real Santa."

"Exactly," Rick said. "He was kind of a ladies' man—but when he was in character, he was all in. The kids loved him and even followed him around the park when we were there."

Rob sat back in his chair. "The only thing I noticed the other day was that he'd lost a lot of weight. He'd taken his padding out when I went to see him, and that suit was hanging on him. It was kind of sad. And his skin was sallower. I was worried he might be sick. But when I asked him about it, he changed the subject."

I remembered something Kane said about diabetes. I wondered just how bad it might be. I needed to keep a list on my phone so I didn't forget who to investigate and what questions I had to remember to ask. "When was the last time you saw him?"

Rob threw his hand up in surrender. "Now you do sound like a cop. It was late afternoon the day he died. I told that woman cop that I was sad that I might have been the last one to see him before his accident. They don't suspect me do they? No one has come around."

He had a grin but his eyes were worried. Talk about micro-expressions. Something was going on here.

"Where did you see him?"

This time he frowned. "In his Santa house. That guy who built it—well, it was the real deal. Davy had come by earlier in the day and asked me to check it out. The place looked like a movie set. It's a shame they had to move it—I mean, I understand why. It's just a shame. It even had a hidden door in the back, so that Santa didn't have to go through the front door. I hope they don't destroy it. Maybe you guys can clean it and use it next year."

I didn't know about that. Having a dead Santa in it was sure to leave some bad juju in there. But he was right. Peggy and Don had worked hard on that house.

A back door? That I hadn't seen, though I honestly didn't look around that much. But what he'd said suggested it might have been Rob I'd seen in the video. And he had left the Santa house through the hidden door.

"Were you by chance wearing a different hoodie that day?"

Rob stared up at the sky, as if he were trying to remember.

His friends laughed. "Rob just puts on what's next in his drawer," Anika said, and then rolled her eyes. "He doesn't pay a lot of attention to what he's actually wearing."

"Harsh, Anika," Rob said, and then snorted as if it was the funniest thing ever. "But she's right. I pretty much wear a black or gray T-shirt and jeans every day. If it's kind of cool, I'll throw on a hoodie. I have a gray, black, and a dark green one."

Oh. No.

It was probably Rob in the hoodie. The timing fit and it hadn't been long after he entered the building that Shannon and I had walked up.

I was about to ask him exactly what time, even though I was pretty sure I knew from the video, when I jumped out of the chair thanks to the blare of a siren and the loudest horn I'd ever heard. A few seconds later, a fire truck pulled up.

And a not too happy Jake stepped out.

What now?

Chapter Twelve

"WHAT ARE YOU doing here?" I asked, as Jake and his men circled the campfire. They were decked out in their full suits and held axes.

"We had a report of a fire here," he said. His voice was gruff and no-nonsense. "Someone drove by and saw the campfire, which isn't allowed in Sweet River's city limits. It's why we have the camp just outside of town."

Rick moved forward. "Technically, we haven't done anything wrong. The fire is in a self-contained pit, which is allowed. I double-checked the rules before we set up here."

Jake wasn't looking at Rick; his eyes were on me. What was he thinking? This was awkward. I'd say my brother had told him to check up on me, but I hadn't said anything to Greg about tonight.

"The person who called it in must have been mistaken about what they saw." He still hadn't taken his eyes off me.

"Well, I certainly don't mind you all stopping by," Anika said. "Big, strong firemen. This night just got a whole lot more fun."

There was some tense laughter.

"Uh. I made a lot of dessert, and there's plenty to go around, if you guys would like some," Anika said. "It's blueberry cobbler."

There was a long pause as Jake's guys looked to him. They never turned down food. Ever. They were always hungry.

"We wouldn't want to interrupt," Jake said, finally tearing his eyes away. He focused on Anika.

"Nah. We were just hanging out," Rob said. "Do you guys know Ainsley? She owns that great shop on Main Street."

The firemen chuckled.

"He's one of my brother's best friends," I said.

Rob glanced from me to Jake, and then back to me. "Huh. Okay great."

"Where's George?" Jake asked me.

"With Shannon and Mike. We'd originally planned to go to Dooley's but he shut down for a family emergency."

His focus moved from me to Rob again, and then back. "His sister is having twins. The whole family went down to Houston to wait it out at the hospital."

"Oh. I had no idea he was going to be an uncle. He'll be a great one."

Dooley was a motorcycle dude who turned home cooking into an art. Which was why many articles and television specials had been made featuring him. While he looked like the gruffest dude on the planet, he was the opposite of that. He just liked to feed people and had a good time with everyone who walked through his door.

Jake's eyebrow went up. Again.

I give up. I had no idea what was happening.

Introductions were made, and then everyone stood around and ate cobbler.

No that wasn't awkward at all. Especially when Jake and Rob started talking about video games like they were best buds.

Ugh.

"I'm going to head out," I whispered to Rob. "I have to teach at the university tomorrow."

He turned away from Jake. "Wait, you still teach?"

"I do. A popular fiction class. It's our last review before finals. I should get going."

"Let me walk you to your car."

"I'll do it," Jake said at the same time.

"It's okay. I'll be fine."

"Nah. Come on," Rob said.

He put his arm around my shoulders as we walked the twenty feet to my car. "I'm sorry about all of this." He waved a hand toward where everyone was standing.

"Don't be. You didn't do anything wrong. I enjoyed meeting your friends—they're really nice people."

"I've never met anyone like you," he said as he opened the door to my SUV.

I laughed. "What do you mean?"

"I don't know, most women would have canceled. I mean, we were supposed to be on a date."

I still wasn't so sure about that. "Oh. Well, stuff happens. And I'm grateful I had a chance to try Rick's shrimp and grits. That was one tasty meal."

I climbed in and turned the car on, welcoming the warmth from the heater.

"I think we should try it again," he said. "The date that is. Maybe next time, we won't be interrupted by your ex."

I laughed. "Ex? How did you—we, uh, it's complicated. He's not—it's too hard to explain. He and my brother, and Kane, who is the ME, are all kind of overprotective."

He chuckled. "I don't know about that. The fireman couldn't take his eyes off you. You might not be interested, but I know that look. He is."

Maybe he was jealous.

He leaned in and kissed my cheek. His lips were warm and nice.

Nice. Ugh. As in, no spark whatsoever.

Figures. Only one man gave me that thousand bees whirring in my stomach feel.

"I'll be around." As I was backing out, Jake was in my rearview and he didn't look happy.

Could he be jealous? That man was hard to read sometimes.

"And you don't care," I said to no one but myself. But I glanced back again and he was still watching me.

Right. Keep telling yourself that, Ains.

None of this mattered. Rob would be gone in a couple of weeks.

I made up my mind right then to invite Rob to Shannon's party. If he was a murderer, it would be a great way for me to get more information from him in a public place.

And if he wasn't Davy's killer, at least I wouldn't be the only single person at Shannon's party.

I had mysteries to solve. Not the least of which was that tiny boy on a bicycle stealing Christmas lights. I needed to start working on that case soon.

And then there was Davy. My gut, and I'd started to

trust it in situations like this, told me he'd been a completely different person with a dangerous sort of life. What if he'd been working for some bad people?

And what if those people had found him?

With that back entrance, the suspects had grown to just about anyone who'd been preparing for the festival. Did my brother know about it?

I'd been thinking about the case, and on autopilot, I nearly forgot to turn off the road to the winery. It was only eight thirty, and as I pulled up in front of Mike's big farmhouse, he, Shannon, and George came down the steps.

"You're back early." She frowned at me. "Was it a bad date?"

George started to run toward me, but I gave him the look. The one that said, "You better not knock me down." He had a habit of doing that. He skidded to a stop and then trotted toward me.

"Good boy." I rubbed his head.

"She's not answering. That means it was a really bad date," Shannon said.

Mike and I laughed. "No. Strange, maybe, but it wasn't bad."

"Is this a conversation you would like to have alone?" Mike asked. Always the gentleman, that one.

"Nah." I told them what happened and then about Jake showing up.

"What do you think, future hubby? Is Jake maybe jealous? Seems like he made up an excuse to interrupt Ains's date."

Mike's eyes went kind of wide, like he'd rather be anywhere else but answering that questions. "You know me," he said. "I'm not big on understanding that sort of thing."

She patted his chest. "True."

"You had to tell me I was in love with you, remember? I couldn't figure out what it was," he said honestly.

It was true and one of my favorite stories. They'd been coming out of a movie in Austin, when he said that he felt like he didn't want to live without her. But he wasn't sure what that meant.

And she'd said, "I love you, too."

"Doesn't matter what Jake, or anyone else, thinks. In addition to needing to talk to more of the booth owners this week, Greg wants me to find the Christmas thief."

I'd only said something to change the subject. My love life, or lack thereof, was not a topic of discussion I enjoyed.

"Christmas thief?" Mike's brow furrowed.

"Someone is stealing bits and pieces of the town's Christmas décor," I said. "I think I have an idea who it is, but it's going to take a minute to figure out how to catch him or her."

"Is it teens? I remember when I was that age, we used to egg each other on to do dumb stuff. I'm sure they don't mean any harm."

"No, I don't think it's teens. The figure I saw on the security tapes was tiny."

Shannon's hand flew to her chest. "Oh. What if it's a kid and his parents can't afford Christmas? Promise me if that's the story, we keep it away from Greg. I'll pay for whatever they took."

That was one of the things I loved about Shannon, she

had a heart that only grew bigger each day I knew her.

"We'll see." Though, when I'd seen that tiny figure, I'd had a lot of the same sort of thoughts.

"If you find out who it is, let me know," she said.

"Or if you need help, I have some extra time," Mike said. "We're selling a lot through our winery gift shop, our distributors, and your store, but I have folks covering a lot of that. I'd do anything not to have to look at one more wedding magazine."

Shannon punched his shoulder. "It will be here before we know it and we don't even have the cake picked out. At least, I have my dress."

I'd been on a couple of tastings with them. Mike liked everything, which left most of the decision making to Shannon. As the maid of honor, I'd also been there when Shannon picked out her amazing dress, which made her look like an ethereal princess. Her fiancé would flip when she came down the aisle.

"You know it will all be perfect," Mike said. "You and I are all that matters." Then he hugged and kissed her.

"Come on, George. Four's a crowd."

They didn't even notice we were gone.

"Someday, George. Maybe, I'll find that. Though, at this point, I'm okay if it's just you and me. Crime-solving buddies until the end."

George woofed.

Once we were home, I texted Greg and asked if he could put more of the security tapes from the festival, and around town, on a safe server.

With George on the end of the couch watching Hallmark Christmas movies—he especially liked the ones by Julie Sherman Wolfe; actually, we both did—I opened the laptop.

First, I did a search on each of the carnival members. Except for social media posts, and the carnival's website, there wasn't much information.

Rob's social media had tons of pictures of him with different women. The weird thing was that his face was partially hidden in every photo. Most of the time with a hoodie or a hat that was positioned just so. Or the women would be in front of him, just showing the top of his head.

He could have been one of those girls-in-every-port guys and he liked to travel. There were several beach party scenes and even a white-water rafting one. But not a single picture showing his full face.

"That's unusual."

Next, I checked the public records site, but nothing came up. This was my brother's case anyway. I just had to figure out a way to let him know about Rob being in the Santa house without Greg going nuts that I'd been out with the guy.

Using the link and password Greg had sent, I was able to get into the videos. There were about 250 hours to watch from the last week.

"This is going to take me until next Christmas." Luckily, my brother had sent a list of decorations that had been taken around town and the dates the owners noticed them missing.

Starting with the first date, and location, I watched several hours of tape. There was nothing on the first day, and I was just about to give up, when I saw an old blue bike parked in front of the drugstore. A few minutes later, a tiny figure hopped on the bike. In the person's hand, he or she held a couple of plastic poinsettias. Just the red leaves, like the bike rider had grabbed them off one of the plastic plants that sat around the fake topiaries at the drugstore.

The face was turned away, but the bike and his or her shape was in full view. The bike was almost too big for the kid to climb on. I'm not good with ages, but this little guy couldn't have been more than seven or eight, maybe even six. But who would let a six-year-old run around by his or herself?

"Poor thing."

George cocked his head to look at me.

"My gut says, this isn't your ordinary thief."

Yes. I talk to my dog—a lot.

George sighed and then turned back to the holiday movie.

It didn't make sense. I rewound the recording. I was fairly certain it was a boy. He struggled to pedal at first and then found his way. I was no closer to seeing his face. Then he stopped suddenly and turned to look at something.

Coming out of the drugstore, was a face I did recognize.

Davy in his Santa suit with padding and everything. He waved at the boy and then handed him candy canes. They chatted for a about a minute, and then the boy took off again.

In his other hand, Davy held a prescription. I couldn't quite read the label. There was a zoom control on the video. I made the piece of film as big as I could without distorting the picture too much.

Lantus. That was the name on the bag's receipt. I

googled it and discovered it was a slow-release diabetes medication.

What if his blood sugar had been low and he'd stumbled? I'd seen that happen in our store with a few folks. We had to sit them down and give them juice.

But Kane had said he'd died on impact, which meant someone had put him back in that chair.

Switching to the video I'd seen earlier, I backed it up to see the person with the hoodie walking in. Rob had admitted to being there. I checked the time stamp, it was a few minutes before four. Don had left about thirteen minutes before the hoodie guy showed up.

That meant Davy had still been alive. Otherwise, whomever it was would have probably run back out.

I don't know why I was relieved that Don didn't do it. I hadn't suspected him—but it was good to see proof.

I backed up the recording again. Rob had that same gait. I'd noticed it when we were walking from Dooley's to my car.

I checked again to see if I could find anything on him. But there was nothing beyond what I'd seen. Not even a résumé or CV online, which was unusual.

Still, it was odd that someone as successful as he was would leave to run a carnie. The story he and Anika had shared almost felt rehearsed in a way. And why did he always hide his face? He was a good-looking guy.

Something just didn't quite fit right.

Maybe there was more to Rob and Davy than the carnie owner had said. Why would Davy have sought him out to see the Santa house if they weren't that close?

All of that warred with the fact that I didn't get that spidey sense feeling around Rob. He seemed like a genuinely nice guy.

Was it awful to make a date with him because I thought he might know something about the case?

Yes. It was.

But the only way I'd get more information was to ask him more about his relationship with Davy.

I picked up my phone.

Up for a holiday party Saturday night? That was very noncommittal. Wasn't exactly asking him on a date.

Yes! he texted back.

After sending him a smiley-face emoji, I pursed my lips. That back entrance to the Santa house was key. I had to see it for myself.

I texted Kane and my brother about the rear entrance, and asked if they had any more info.

Good to know. Kane texted back. *Still waiting on labs. Holidays suck.*

Then Kane texted me privately. *Sugars were extremely low at time of death. I'll know more in a couple of days.*

I had to laugh.

Poor guy didn't want my brother knowing he'd shared information. If something took too long, he'd run the tests at a lab in Austin himself. But he'd been backlogged. As sad as it is to say, the elderly didn't always seem to fare well around the holidays. We'd had a high number of deaths in the county, most Kane attributed to natural causes, but he had to check them all out.

If Davy was unsteady on his feet because his sugars were

low, it might have been easier for someone to push him.

The candy canes—had he been trying to get his sugars back up? It was a possibility.

But the big question was who knew about that entrance? Other than Rob?

There was no telling who had gone in and out that back entrance. Since the cameras were focused on the main fairway, there wasn't any way to see who might have come in that way.

"George, we have way too many suspects. Even if Davy stumbled because of low blood sugar, someone shoved him back in that chair."

And I may have just had a date with one of those suspects.

Chapter Thirteen

AT THE COLLEGE the next day, the tension was palpable. My class on popular fiction was a fun one, but my tests were not the easiest, and we covered a lot of material over the semester. When we were done with the review, I sat down on the table at the front of the lecture hall to take any last-minute questions.

The class had grown over the last several semesters—I guess, thanks to word of mouth from my former students. I had almost thirty this time, which had meant a whole lot of grading. But it was fun discussing books with young minds and hearing their perspectives.

"This is our last time to meet and I wanted to thank you all for our lively discussions. I hope you all have had as much fun as I have."

They nodded. It really was a great group.

"You can take your test anytime online between Thursday and Saturday. You'll get an extra ten points if you take it before midnight Friday. Grades will be posted online on Monday.

"It's timed. Know that going in. I don't mind if you use your books. If you want to complete the test in time, though, you'll need to know what we reviewed today."

The university liked us to use online testing when possible, so that everything was recorded. It was a way for the university to keep track of things and cut down on student complaints.

While the online test gave them an overall score, the essay questions, which were half the grade, were something that I'd need to read. I waved goodbye as they filed out.

I enjoyed teaching, especially this particular class. We'd had a lot of fun.

A few minutes later, I unlocked the door to the small office the university gave me. I was only here for an hour or two a week. That way the kids could ask questions in private if they wanted.

I'd just sat down, and George settled in the corner on the bed I had there, when my former students Jeff and Lily popped their heads in the door.

"Ms. McGregor, how are you?" Lily asked, as she and Jeff moved to sit in the chairs in front of my desk.

"It's good to see you two. How was your semester? Did you miss me?"

"We did," Lily said. "We heard a rumor that you might be teaching a creative writing class in addition to the popular fiction one. It doesn't have an instructor listed on the online catalog and we were curious if that rumor was true."

These two were some of the brightest students I'd ever had.

"Can you keep a secret?"

They glanced at one another and then me, and nodded.

I laughed. "The rumor is true. The dean asked if I could take over the creative fiction class while Dr. Elizabeth Bailey is on maternity leave next semester. I have enough people working at the store, so I'm pretty sure I can swing it."

"Yay!" Lily said as she clapped her hands. "We're both going to sign up for that one. And we were curious if you might need a couple of TAs for the popular fiction class. We know the materials."

Well, that would be great, especially with the extra class. I'd have a lot more reading to do with the creative writing class.

"Let me talk to the dean. If she says it's okay, I'd love to have both of you as TAs. They may even be able to provide a small stipend but I make no promises in that regard."

"We don't care about the money, we've just learned a lot from you." Lily pulled her hair up into a ponytail. She was a striking young woman. She and Jeff had been best friends since they were freshmen.

"Any plans for the holidays?" Jeff asked.

"Working at the shop and the festival." Once I was through the holiday season, I'd be sleeping for a couple of weeks. The weekend after Christmas, we'd be open only on Saturday to sell off any leftover holiday items. Then we'd be closed the first two weeks of January, to restock and clean up the store before we headed into the Valentine's season.

All of us needed that break and I was very much looking forward to it.

"But I don't think you care about my holiday plans or being teacher's assistants." I smirked.

Jeff and Lily glanced at one another again.

"We really are interested in being TAs for you. Lily's right, we learn a lot from you," Jeff said.

"But we read the paper," they said at the same time.

"I mean, a dead Santa—that's all kinds of wrong." Jeff's face was priceless, his eyes wide and his head shaking.

"That's because you still believe in Santa," Lily interjected.

I chuckled.

Jeff gave her a mean look and then grinned. "My mom and dad don't do presents at my house unless you believe in Santa."

This time we all laughed.

"The newspaper said the case was a suspicious death. We are here for whatever you need."

I was about to say, 'no,' but stopped myself.

"You guys know I can't talk about my brother's case. Other than it's an active investigation and there's a lot of suspects. Pretty much, anyone who was around that day could have done it. But I could use your assistance with another case," I said. "One that is equally mystifying. That is if you aren't too busy studying for finals."

Lily shook her head. "We opted out of our finals—our grades were high enough."

Of course they did. Some professors gave that option, but I wasn't one of them. "Why am I not surprised?" These two were exceptionally bright and they had a way of looking at evidence from a different perspective.

"What have you got for us?" Jeff asked. "We can start right away if you want."

I told them about the Christmas thief.

"It's not as exciting as murder," Lily said.

I rolled my eyes.

"But it's interesting that it might be a kid, especially

since he keeps getting away with it," Jeff said. "It has to be someone no one would suspect or they'd have caught him by now."

Lily nodded.

"Why don't you two come by the shop tomorrow, and I'll show you the video." This was the first time Greg had trusted me with something like this but I didn't think he'd mind if Lily and Jeff were involved.

I think the saving grace for me, was that his already stretched resources were even thinner with the festival going on for the next couple of weeks and his multitude of other cases in the county.

"We're happy to do it," Lily said. "But if you hear anything about the Santa case, will you tell us? Any theories?"

It was definitely murder. Maybe one that had not been premeditated but when opportunity arose, someone took advantage of it.

"The victim had a medical condition. But that's all I can say. You two come by the store this evening, and I'll share whatever I can with you, and show you the video."

I had to talk to the women who knew Davy the best. What if Caroline hadn't liked the fact he'd been hanging out with Mary Beth?

The two women were friendly. I'd seen that on the video when they hugged.

I couldn't imagine tiny Caroline shoving anyone hard enough to do that kind of damage.

That reminded me, as much as it pained me to go back in that Santa house, I had to take a look inside. And I had to talk to Don and Peggy again. They and Mary Beth had talked about his expertise with contracts and such.

I was into my thoughts, and it took a good minute to realize the kids had left.

After waiting another half hour to see if any of my students had questions, I locked up the office and piled George into my car.

"George, I think it's time we took a look at Santa's house. I just have to figure out where it is."

"Ruurrrhuu."

"I'm excited too."

The killer had slipped out the hidden door. There were a few people at the top of my list: Rob, Caroline and Mary Beth. There was no way Don and Peggy—who'd also known about the secret door—could have done this. And he now had a good alibi.

I didn't want it to be any of them—especially the guy I'd asked out.

˷

AN HOUR LATER, George and I pulled up into the impound lot. There was a guard there, and he eyed me suspiciously.

"Civilians are not allowed in here," he said angrily. I didn't know who he was, but he'd definitely woken up on the wrong side of the bed.

"If you're picking up an impounded vehicle, you need to go around the corner to the station." We were far outside of Sweet River, almost to Warrenton, which was where the sheriff's department kept everything they'd impounded in a ginormous warehouse I hadn't even known existed.

I held up my driver's license. "I'm meeting my brother, here. He's the sheriff." If I believed that might grant me some favor, I was wrong. It didn't seem to matter to him, who my brother might be.

"Stay here," he grumbled.

I texted Greg that I was having trouble getting in.

After going back into his guard shack, and talking on a walkie-talkie, he came back.

He handed me a clipboard to sign. "You have to sign in and out. Your vehicle may be searched at any time. As a civilian, you are not allowed to touch any of the evidence. Your dog can't get out of the car; it might contaminate any evidence we're holding here."

George grunted as if he was offended, and it was all I could do not to laugh. That dog understood everything. Like, everything. It was uncanny sometimes.

"Okay." George wouldn't mind. We'd taken a walk at the university and he'd just stretched out to take a nap in the back of my SUV. It was a chilly day, so I didn't have to worry about him getting too hot.

After driving through the gate, I followed the arrows until I found Greg's Expedition parked at the end of the metal warehouse. All the way down the road were boats and fancy sports cars. The majority of vehicles were nicer than anything I'd ever driven. Though, I loved my red Explorer. It was just the right size for George and me.

Greg was dressed in jeans and a button-down. I'd noticed the last few months he'd been wearing his sheriff's uniform, less and less. I wondered if that was to make people feel like he was more accessible. Though, he'd always been friendly with the townspeople. As much as I hated to admit it, my brother was a great guy and well respected.

"Hey, George," he walked over to pat my dog's head through the window, which made George very happy.

"Thanks for including me," I said. When I'd texted Greg before leaving the school, he'd said he and Lucy and Kane were already there and they'd wait for me. "The guard at the gate said George had to stay in the car." After making sure the windows were open, I stepped out.

He nodded. "Probably, best. I have to do everything by the book, again, since you found the body. We have to worry about contamination. That means you need to wear these when we get inside." He handed me the footy things that fit over my shoes, and a pair of gloves.

"No problem. George, I'll be right back. If you stick your head out the window you can see me." I pointed toward the warehouse, which had a large sliding door that was already open.

George grunted and then lay down in the seat. One of the reasons I didn't leave him alone very often was that he had abandonment issues. His original owner had died, and no one realized it for several days.

That would scar anyone, especially a young puppy. If he was away from me for too long, he grew incredibly anxious. Which is why I was always hitting up my friends as dog-sitters.

Inside the warehouse, Santa's house was on prominent display right inside the doors. Funny, how much smaller it appeared in this huge warehouse. There were a couple of yachts, and some super fancy cars down to the left.

"Uh." What was all this stuff doing in Greg's impound lot?

"Yep. Nuts. I know. Something you would not expect. You cannot say anything about what you see in here," he said. "A lot of it is part of ongoing investigations where drugs are involved."

I sometimes forgot that my brother dealt with more than small-town politics. There had been a restructuring of the counties in regard to law enforcement, and he was now over a couple of different counties, and worked with local and state officials on several cases.

"We have a lake, but they aren't big enough for those big yachts."

"I can't talk about it, Ains. I mean it. You can't say a word. I'm breaking protocol as it is. But I trust your gut. Lean on me, to put your covers on."

I did what he asked and then put on the gloves.

"Let's go," he said.

Inside Santa's house, there were two familiar faces: Kane and Lucy. They were talking as they tapped on the walls.

They turned toward us as we walked in the double doors. Most of the cheery decorations were still here, as was Santa's throne.

But the wood floor was covered with a huge bloodstain, and the North Pole sign was missing.

I shivered. This was no longer a happy place.

"Do you know where the secret door is?" Kane asked. "Lucy and I have been all over the place, a half dozen times."

"Yep. I called Don when I was on the way over. He told me how to do it."

Don was angry with himself for not thinking about it.

I stepped carefully over the cute reindeer and elves behind the throne, nearly tripping on a string of lights I hadn't seen. "It's dark in here. I can't really see very well," I said, catching myself on the back wall. Oops. At least, I'd worn the gloves.

A blinding light flashed on and I had to blink the stars away from my eyes. "Warn me next time," I grumbled.

My brother held one of his search lights from his sheriff's vehicle, which pretty much illuminated the whole structure. I found Rudolph's tail, and pushed it in. A panel slid across the back wall, and there was an opening.

"Don't move," Kane yelled. "There may be trace evidence." He crawled over the animatronic figures, the same way I did. Then he took out swabs and plastic baggies. It was as if I didn't exist. The man had a passion for his work, that was for sure.

"How did we all miss this?" Lucy asked Greg. "Why didn't Mr. Clark tell us about it? I find that suspicious."

Greg shook his head. "It wasn't Don, Lucy. You have to trust me on that."

"Hold on a second," I said. I pulled out my phone and dialed Don.

"Morning, Ainsley, were you able to get the door open?" Don asked.

I had it on speaker so everyone could hear. "We did. I was curious if you'd mentioned that door to anyone else? Or if Davy had said who he had told?"

"Let me think. I can't believe I forgot to tell the police. I was in shock and I still don't have my brain back."

"I understand. Take a second and think about your conversation with him when you showed him what you'd built."

"He was in a great mood. We talked about him coming out to stay with us. I asked about his diet. He'd lost a good hundred and fifty pounds. He said he'd been kind of sick, but he was better. Oh. He said he wanted to text his friends about the door. I bet if you checked his phone you could see who he told. I didn't mention it to anyone else, I don't think. But I'll keep thinking."

"Thanks. Tell Ms. Peggy I said hello. And I'll be back to the shop in just a bit."

I hung up.

"Anyone could have come in or gone out this way, not just that guy in the hoodie," Lucy said. They *had* seen the security tape. "Also, it explains how the suspect left." She turned to me. "How did you find out about it?"

"I need some more evidence bags," Kane said. "I've found several different fibers here. We need to get them to a lab."

"I'll get them," Lucy said as she walked out.

"I'd like to know the answer," Greg said. "Did Don tell you?"

I glanced down at Rudolph.

"Ains?"

"No. I heard it from someone I talked to at the festival."

"You understand, whoever it is, just became our prime suspect."

Oh. Man. I did not want to hear the lecture that was about to come my way.

"No. I don't understand. It could have been anyone. You

heard what Don said. Davy texted his friends to tell them about it. You just need to look at his phone."

"We didn't find one," Greg said. "All of his belongings were in his vehicle but it wasn't there either."

"Did you guys find out who he really is? I still think he might be a lawyer. I mean who else knows stuff about contracts?"

My brother put his hands on his hips. "Tell me."

He wasn't going to be fooled by me trying to change the subject.

"Like I was saying, Davy thought it was cool that Don had put in the secret door. He was showing a lot of people that day. He was really proud of what Don had done."

"Okay," he said softly, "but who told you about the door?"

I sighed. "Rob."

"Who's that?"

"The guy I had a date with last night."

Chapter Fourteen

On Tuesday morning, I met Armand and Justin at Shannon's coffee house at nine in the morning. I'd already made sure the shop was ready to go, as Tuesday is my day to open and I had about an hour before I needed to get back.

After getting our drinks, we walked back to my shop for privacy. The coffee shop was crowded and this town had ears everywhere. My plan was to ask them more about the love triangle that was Davy, Mary Beth, and Caroline. But this was also about business. I wanted to show them where we could put a booth for their German Christmas ornaments.

"Did you hear the big news?" Justin asked.

"My husband is a gossip." Armand snorted.

"That's okay, he'll fit right in with the folks in this town."

We all chuckled.

I'd left George with Mike, who was restocking his wine booth in Bless Your Art. He had a cooler with artisanal cheeses in his display that were my kryptonite. I was always buying them when I forgot my lunch. His friend mixed Mike's wine in with goat cheese—best stuff ever.

"We can sit here." I motioned them toward the table in the break room at the back of the store.

George woofed and trotted toward us.

"I meant to tell you the other day what a gorgeous dog he is," Armand said. That English accent of his made everything sound like a compliment.

"He must eat buckets of food," Justin added.

"He's a big guy, but he only eats a couple of large bowls a day. Though, he's partial to people food. But that happened long before we rescued each other."

"Oh, I love rescue stories," Justin said. "God bless you for taking him in."

"Like I said, we rescued each other. I'm more grateful to George than anyone will ever know." He'd been my faithful companion and except for his abandonment anxiety, penchant for chasing squirrels and at the same time being extremely lazy, he was nearly perfect. "What was it you were going to tell me?"

"No one can find Caroline. All of her stuff is in her booth, and her camper is still at the site, but no one has seen her since Sunday night."

Armand rolled his eyes. "She probably went home to get more stock. We have to do the same thing tomorrow. This event has been incredibly successful. Thanks to you, my dear. We need to check on the shop. We left Justin's brother in charge and we never know if he's going to show up."

Justin laughed. "He's right. My brother lives in a world where time is relative. But he's aces when it comes sales. He could sell duck fat to ducks. Luckily, we also have an assistant manager, who is amazing. I'm sure she and the rest of the staff have things handled.

"Anyway… No one has seen or heard from Caroline."

"How do you know she's disappeared?"

"Her car is gone, but nothing else."

Something twisted in my gut and bile rose in my throat. "Did anyone check inside her camper?"

"No," Armand said. "Since her car was gone, we assumed she left. And her camper door was locked."

"I did try to peek in the windows, just to make sure she wasn't sick," Justin said. "That was before we figured out her car was gone. Normally, though, when someone takes off, they let the rest of us know. That way we can keep an eye on things for them."

"Were you able to see in the windows?"

Justin sighed. "No. She has the ones that are really high up, and our ladder was here at our booth. But we banged pretty hard on her door. There wasn't an answer."

Huh.

What if the killer thought Caroline knew too much? She'd spent a lot of time with the victim. It wasn't really a stretch. Or maybe she was the killer, and was on the run.

I'd make a trip out to the campground to see if I could figure out what was going on.

The guys and I decided on a consignment deal.

In a half hour we were done. I headed out to the campground, which actually took me right past my place. I stopped, and grabbed the small stepladder I kept in the barn, and then went on.

There were several roads around the lake that branched out. The first one took me to the campsite where I found the silver Airstream trailer with the mermaid on the door that the guys had mentioned.

I had imagined there would be people milling around, but there weren't. It was too quiet—like, even the birds weren't chirping.

This was all kinds of weird. I kind of wished I'd brought George with me. But he'd been napping behind the counter and I didn't want to bug him.

After walking around the camper a couple of times and not really seeing anything unusual, I opened the back of my SUV, to pull out the ladder.

A shiver ran down my spine and I glanced around to see if someone was watching me. They might think I was trying to break in. But I had to make sure Caroline wasn't lying in her trailer in a pool of blood.

There. I thought it out loud. The picture burned in my brain as soon as the guys had mentioned she was missing. Maybe I should have tried the door first, but I worried I might mess up fingerprints.

I sat the ladder down near the front windows of the camper trailer. A twig snapped behind me and I whirled around.

No one was there.

"Hello? Is someone out here?"

Dead silence.

Dead being the operative word there.

"It's not going to get any less creepy." I said it out loud, more to break the silence than anything.

I climbed to the top of the ladder and then on my tippy toes, I used my hand to shade my eyes and peek in.

The whole place was in disarray. I didn't know Caroline very well, but she'd been extremely put together and her booth organized and pristine.

But her trailer looked as though someone had been trying to find something. Clothes were strewn all over the floor and the bedding was in a pile.

I could see everything through the window, except the bathroom. Or what I assumed to be a bathroom or closet. The door was shut.

What if the killer put her in there?

I picked up my phone and texted Greg.

GREG CALLED LATE that afternoon. I was in the back of the store putting together the bank deposit. During the holidays we were doing twice-a-day runs so we didn't have too much cash around.

While most people used credit cards these days, older people shopped early and used cash. We'd had several groups of ladies come through, which was why I hadn't been able to stay at the campground and check on the progress of Caroline's whereabouts earlier.

"What's up?" I answered.

"We checked her camper and she's not there," he said. "The place is a mess. And we are taking forensic evidence just in case. But it looks more like she just left in a hurry. I thought you might want to know. Technically, she's not even a missing person yet."

I sighed. "She was dating the victim. She said she'd been in her camper working on projects, but no one saw her there. I was worried she might have done a runner. Or that the killer was after her. Then there's the whole thing where the victim might have also been, uh, dating her friend. I don't know. She doesn't seem like the killer type, and she isn't big enough to have shoved him—I'm rambling. I just want to make sure she's all right."

His voice warbled as if he held his hand over his phone. "Lucy says, officers checked her residence and there's no sign of her there. Maybe, she just went shopping."

But she'd been gone a long time and her booth at the festival was shut up tight. I couldn't imagine she'd miss out on sales, even though it wasn't that busy on a Tuesday. "Okay, it just seems odd that a woman, traveling alone, wouldn't tell her friends she was leaving. I had one of my feelings that things might be hinky."

"I've got to go. Kane's calling."

"Wait a—"

He hung up. Obviously, he was annoyed with me for wasting time and resources when he was already stretched thin. But my gut still said something was fishy. It was nearly closing time, and it dawned on me that Mary Beth had never come up to talk about her quilts.

Maybe she changed her mind.

I texted her and waited. No answer. I took a quick peek out the back door and walked down the path. A few of the other booths were closed, including hers. Neither she nor Caroline were working. Maybe they'd gone somewhere together.

Or Caroline killed Mary Beth.

My stomach churned with worry.

I texted Armand to ask if he'd seen Mary Beth.

No. Maybe she and Caroline are together?
Oh. My.

I put the money and checks in the deposit bag, and then texted Mike. He and Don had been taking turns doing the runs.

"Hey, Ains," Mike said from the doorway. "Have you got it ready?"

I handed him the bag. "You know, I can do this."

He offered a bemused grin. "We just feel safer with the tourists in town if Don and I do it. I was stocking the shelves anyway. Second time today, which is always welcome news. Looks like the last of the customers just checked out. Do you want me to lock up?"

I glanced at the clock. It was five. We closed early on Tuesday and Wednesday, because there usually wasn't that much traffic on those days.

"I'll do it. Thank you."

He snapped his fingers. "Oh. I need best-friend guidance."

I had a feeling what he was about to ask. "Didn't we have this same conversation around this time last year?"

He laughed. "Yes, and you were a godsend. Do you have any ideas for this year?"

"Shannon, loves you. Anything you get her will be perfect."

"I know. But I like to keep things…fresh. I don't want to do the expected. She's not really into the easy stuff like jewelry."

Easy stuff. I snorted. I guess it was easier for a guy to go into a jewelry store and have a sales clerk pick out a gift. I mean, I wouldn't mind a diamond or four. But Shannon wasn't like me.

"They are kind of pricey, but last time we were at Junk Gypsies, she was eyeing a great pair of painted peacock boots. She would love those, and she'd think you were a psychic for knowing she wanted them."

"I knew you'd come up with a good idea. Any chance you could print a picture for me? And I'm embarrassed to say I don't know what size she wears."

After printing off the page on the Junk Gypsy site, I handed it to him. "She wears a size eight. Hold on just a second."

I glanced at the clipboard I'd been using to check off the owners of the booths I'd visited. "Tomorrow, go to booth sixty-three. It's down toward where the carnival rides are. The lady there makes stunning jewelry."

"But..."

"She may not be into diamonds and gold. But that woman had dangling peacock earrings made out of silver, lapis, turquoise and some onyx, I think. I was actually going to pick those up for her, but you could do a theme gift."

"You're brilliant, Ains. Thanks."

"You're welcome."

A few minutes later, I walked to the front of the store to lock the front door. George didn't even bother to follow. He was nice and warm next to the heater in my office.

Mrs. Whedon was sitting at the front counter knitting what looked like an afghan. It was a gorgeous cerulean.

"Are you making that for someone in particular?" It was a cable knit and kind of looked like a huge sweater blanket.

"I'm trying out a new cable stitch, why?" She was a curmudgeonly soul, but a few months ago, I'd cleared her name for a crime she did not commit, and she'd been overly nice to me. Every once in a while, I'd find fresh bread, or a pie in the office courtesy of her talented self. But if I tried to say thanks, she'd get cranky and shoo me away.

"That's my favorite color. I was wondering if I can buy it when you're done. It'd go great in my living room."

"Well, that's good, since it's your Christmas present. I'm your Secret Santa."

I laughed. We'd all picked names the day before Thanksgiving and would reveal ourselves at the Christmas party I planned to throw for everyone. "So, much for the secret part."

Her lips quirked up on the right side. "It's silly nonsense, but everyone else was participating, and I didn't want to be a jerk."

She'd lived a lot of years, and as far as I knew, didn't do anything she didn't want to these days. She had no filters and didn't suffer fools.

"Well, I couldn't be happier to know that's coming my way and I'm grateful you participated in our gift exchange. I like doing things that bring us all together."

She gave a weary sigh. "That's why I did it. I could tell it was important to you."

I adored her. Grumpy as she was, she could be a dear. "But your gift is extravagant. Our limit is $40."

"Instead of buying you a bunch of crap that you'll never use, I gave myself a discount on the yarn. I won't be over the budget."

She had an answer for everything. I'm really glad she didn't go to jail for a murder she didn't commit.

"I'm going to head out. Can I give you a ride home?" After she knocked down her third parking meter on Main Street, we'd all been taking turns. She kept telling us she just needed new glasses, but she was well into her eighties, and didn't need to be out on the road.

I'm not ageist, she just had a really bad driving record. My brother Greg had begged me to find a way to get her off the streets.

She's super quick and smart. Just her eyesight isn't what it used to be—even with the glasses she'd just bought a couple of months ago.

She pulled up a large tote bag that was on the floor by her feet and stuffed the yarn and needles in it. "I'm not a charity case," she said.

"Of course, you aren't. I need your brain."

She gave me a look that said she didn't believe me.

"Kane has ruled Santa's death as suspicious circumstances, which most likely means murder."

Her eyes lit up. No way she'd ever admit she loved solving crimes, even when she was the suspect, but she had a different way of looking at the world and people that I appreciated. "Should we get out the murder board?"

That's all I needed, half the town knowing I had all kinds of suspects and a Santa who wasn't who he said he was. No one knew that except for law enforcement, Don and Peggy, Shannon, and me, and I planned to keep it that way.

"Can't. And it isn't just because Greg might kill me. We have a lot more people coming through the store, and we shouldn't risk someone seeing it." And Greg *would* kill me—not literally of course. But who wanted to listen to my old hen of a brother nagging? Not. Me.

That reminded me, Jeff and Lily had never made it by to look at the video. I'd check on them later.

Mrs. Whedon followed George and me out the back door. "Do you mind stopping at the Dairy Queen?" she asked. "I want a chicken sandwich."

It was the opposite way from taking her home, but I never minded going to DQ.

"No problem."

"Who are your suspects?"

"Will you promise to keep it on the down low?"

She smirked. "I'm not Helen and Erma. I can keep a secret."

"Well, he was seeing a couple of different women. Both of whom seem to be missing at the moment."

"Missing?"

I explained what I knew. "And several people who are here travel around together to different events. They knew the victim, at least over the last year. And then there's Don and Peggy, who were best friends with him years ago."

"You don't suspect them do you? Those are two of the kindest souls I've ever met, sometimes to their own detriment."

I pulled into the takeout line at the DQ. It was long, and it seemed like everyone else in town had the same idea.

"No. I don't. You were there when Don saw his friend—he was genuinely excited to see him. And he's devastated over his death. They'd just reconnected."

"Good. I was upset with your brother for bringing him in."

"That whole thing got out of hand. All they did was ask Don to come in and answer a few questions, because they had nothing to go on. It was all about getting background info on the victim. At the time, we didn't even know he'd been dating anyone."

"If he was dating more than one woman, it could be jealousy."

I nodded. "I've met two of the women," I said. "They are nice and seem to be friends with each other. They are genuinely upset over his death. You're right, though. Jealousy can make people do awful things."

"Before he was Santa, what did he do?"

I bit my lip. "We don't know. Not even Don and Peggy do. They all met at a Santa Claus convention years ago. He traveled a lot, like all over the world. But they said he never really talked about himself."

"He was hiding his past. Did he have an alias?"

Argh.

"Um," I said.

"That's a yes, then. Technically, you didn't tell me so the sheriff can't say a word. Have you searched on your computer?"

"Welcome to Dairy Queen. Can I take your order?" the box on the sign in the drive-thru said.

After asking for a chicken finger basket, a chicken sandwich meal, and a couple of burgers for George, we waited to pay.

"I went through some old letters of Don and Peggy's.

I'm not really sure when or what to search for to be honest. Most of what he said was about his travels and there were very few personal details."

"Do you have any clues to the past? Anything you might have heard?"

I tapped my finger on the steering wheel, thinking back over the last few days. "He was a jack of all trades. Like, pretty good at a lot of different stuff. He'd assisted one of the women with contracts. Maybe he was a lawyer or a businessman. But without a name—it's tough to search. Greg is using the FBI's resources to do facial recognition, but nothing has come up. I mean, everyone in law enforcement seems to be moving slow after Thanksgiving. Maybe, we'll get an answer this week."

We were quiet on the way to her house. When we arrived, I jumped out to open her door and lend a hand. She shooed me away. "I'm not an invalid," she said as she climbed out and then turned to grab her bag.

She headed toward the big front porch of her white cottage. It was a cool old house with a lot of detailed woodwork, and everything from the paint to the flowerbeds was pristine. She put the rest of us to shame.

I waited for her to go inside, but she turned. "Maybe, try looking for big cases a few months before Don and Peggy met him. Seems to me, he was hiding something. And a Santa disguise is perfect. Maybe a lawyer, businessman, or accountant. Could be he was a nice guy who got mixed up with the wrong crowd."

"But where to search? He could have been anywhere in the world, before they met in Minnesota."

She winked at me. "You and I both know that people try to stick close to home when they can. I'd start close to Minnesota, and then branch out. Good night, Ainsley. Thanks for the food. It's my cheat day and I really wanted a chicken sandwich."

Cheat day? I laughed. In her eighties, and still looking after herself. "You're welcome."

My phone rang as I pulled out of her driveway. "Ainsley?"

It was Don. "Is everything okay?"

"Yes," he said. "I was wondering if you could stop by for a minute. We found old photos of Don and us, and we thought they might be good for the investigation. He looked really different back then."

I'm not sure why they didn't call my brother or Lucy. "Okay. We should probably get them to the police."

"I called the station and your brother and Lucy are out on a case. I was worried if I just left them there, they might get lost."

"I'll be there in just a bit. And thank you. I know how hard all of this must be for you two."

There was silence for a minute.

"It is. But someone hurt Davy and we will do whatever it takes to get him justice."

I was definitely on board with that.

∽

FIVE HOURS LATER, I was still on the couch with my laptop. I hadn't found anything about a big court case or arrests for around that time in Minnesota or Wisconsin. I'd tried Ohio. My eyeballs were dry from staring at the screen. I was about to give up, when my Google page loaded. There were several big cases that had to do with money laundering.

There was one article where a picture of a large man with a black hood over his head was being ushered into a courtroom.

Same height as Davy, and the perfect body shape for a Santa. Could that be him?

I picked up the pictures Don had given me. Yes, I could have dropped them by the station but I hadn't wanted to go all the way back into town.

I had texted Greg that I had them.

Holding one of pictures up next to my computer, I made the photo larger on my screen. Definitely a fit for the body type.

It was a long shot, but I kept reading to see if they mentioned the guy's name. He was just called the forensic accountant. But his body type wouldn't be easy to hide, if he'd been working for those involved in the case—he'd be easily recognizable.

If it was him.

For five minutes, I debated whether to call Greg. I didn't want to listen to him yell at me for sending him on another wild-goose chase. But my gut churned. This was our guy. It had to be.

To avoid the yelling, I copied and pasted the link into a text to Kane and Greg.

After letting George out for his last break, I locked all the doors and windows.

If I was right, and the people he'd informed on more than twenty years ago had found him, that would be a great motive for murder. In the movies, professional hits are often made to look like accidents.

I flipped on the porch light, just as George gave a menacing growl. Someone knocked lightly on the door and I jumped.

Chapter Fifteen

AFTER FINALLY CATCHING my breath, I peeked through the glass to see Jeff and Lily standing on my porch.

I'm going to kill them.

"It's okay, George. Just friends."

He moseyed off the couch to stand by me as I opened the door.

"What are you guys doing here this late? You scared me to death."

Lily cringed. "We're sorry. The light was on, and we thought we'd knock softly to see if you were still awake."

"I am now," I said. It wasn't their fault I was on edge. "Sorry. I just was expecting you at the shop."

Jeff sighed. "We're the ones who are sorry. All the dorms were on lockdown. Someone called in a bomb threat. My guess is it was a fake one to get out of taking finals. We have at least one call every semester around this time. But they have to take them seriously. If it's too late, we can meet with you tomorrow."

My heart beat fast and there was no way I'd be going to bed anytime soon.

George licked Lily's hand. He liked everyone except bad guys but he had a special fondness for her.

"It's okay. Come on in. Do you guys want hot chocolate?

And I have leftover pie."

Jeff's eyes lit up.

"We don't want you to go to any trouble," Lily said, as she pet George's head. He was in heaven.

"It's no trouble."

"I never turn down real food." Jeff rubbed his belly. "We missed the cafeteria because of the lockdown."

I ushered them inside and had them sit at the kitchen bar while I cut the pie and made the hot chocolate.

"Do you want a turkey sandwich? I have leftovers."

They both nodded.

I remembered what it was like eating dorm food for several months.

After putting everything together, and letting George outside, I grabbed my laptop and sat it on the bar.

"Here's the video I wanted to show you."

They watched it a couple of times.

"He's tiny." Lily leaned in and shifted her glasses on top of her head.

"How do you know it's a he?"

She pointed at the video. "He's shaped like my little brother and is even wearing the same kind of jeans. I mean, it could be a girl. It's hard to tell because the hoodie is always up but I think it's boy."

She was really good at this.

"Our best bet would be to check the bike racks at the elementary schools," I said. "Not in a creepy stalker way. And then if you find it, give me a call. I can follow him home. Again, not in a creepy stalker way. I just don't have time to check the schools for the bike."

We laughed.

"It's sad, though." Lily frowned. "If he's stealing, maybe his family can't afford Christmas decorations. He has to be a first grader, or a very small second grader."

She was right. I sighed. It twisted my soul that this little guy was having to create his own Christmas.

"We want to make sure he's not alone."

Lily sniffed. "Oh, that would be terrible. What if he's having to take care of himself?"

I hoped that wasn't true but I was worried about the same thing.

"Don't worry, Lily, we'll find him tomorrow, I promise," Jeff said and then patted Lily's shoulder. There was nothing sexual between them. They were just friends but I loved how they looked out for one another.

"Thank you, both. Just do me a favor and don't spook him. The last thing I want to do is terrify the poor kid."

Lily pursed her lips. "Ms. McGregor, if we find him, will the sheriff…"

I shook my head. "Don't worry about that. My brother may not seem like it, but he has a big, mushy heart just like mine. We'll figure it all out."

She let out a breath.

"We have to get back," Jeff said. "Because of what happened there's a curfew starting at midnight. We'll let you know."

They stood. "Hold on." Quickly, I put the remaining pie in a container. "You guys can share this."

Jeff's grin widened. "Thank you."

I chuckled. "You're welcome." Better to feed a growing

young adult rather than pile more weight on my hips.

"And gang, in the future...maybe shoot me a text before you come over? I never mind you visiting. But this way you don't scare me to death."

"Noted," Jeff said, and then they both waved goodbye.

After they left, George was ready to pass out.

But my mind whirred with questions. Who was that little boy? And was he safe?

Chapter Sixteen

Normally, George liked to sleep on the couch, but I'd been creeped out the night before that assassins might be in town. Sweet River wasn't that kind of place but then we'd never had an informant murdered here before. I mean, if I was right about all of that. My gut said I was.

Whoever had killed him probably wouldn't have stuck around. But I never assumed anything anymore. Especially, after I'd seen all those cars and boats that had been confiscated at the warehouse. Whatever was going on with that case, it had to be nearby or that stuff wouldn't have been there.

I shivered.

I liked to think our sweet little town was a safe haven but bad stuff could happen anywhere. I, of all people, should know that.

I was just about to roll out of bed because George was doing his I-have-to-pee-now whine. Someone banged loudly on my door. It was seven thirty. Who would be visiting at this hour? I stumbled down the stairs after George, who barked excitedly.

I glanced down to make sure I at least had clothes on. I did. I wore my *I'm Not Adulting Today* T-shirt and bright pink unicorn pajama pants.

It would do.

The door is paned glass with intricate wood detailing, making it easy to see who was on my porch.

People showing up uninvited was evidently a regular thing around here.

"You could have called," I said and then motioned for Greg and Lucy to come in.

"I've been trying, but you didn't answer."

I glanced at the couch, where my phone lay next to the laptop.

"I was doing what most people do this time of morning. I was sleeping."

"Do you have that coffee you bought in Austin?" my brother asked, plowing forward into my kitchen.

George sat staring at Lucy.

"Why is your dog looking at me like that?" she asked quietly.

I laughed. "He needs to go outside. If you let him out the back door, he'll be your best friend for life."

Her eyebrow rose. "Come on boy. Outside," she said in her no-nonsense way. George trotted after her.

"Thank God." Greg started the coffee maker.

"Is everything okay?" Now that my eyes weren't fuzzy with sleep, I noticed he winced at the light.

"Damn headache," he said.

"He's allergic to the Christmas tree he bought," Lucy offered, and then laughed. "But he refuses to get rid of it because he likes the smell."

I started giggling. "Greg, our whole family is allergic to pine trees. Why didn't you get a fake one?"

"They didn't have any left. And I like live trees, so sue

me."

I grabbed a box of Mucinex and Excedrin Migraine from the pantry where I kept meds. "Take one each of these. After a couple of cups of coffee, you'll have the energy of a thousand bees when that double dose of caffeine hits and you'll feel a lot better."

He popped the pills in his mouth.

Then we all stood there staring at one another.

"Uh?" I raised my hands like what's up. And then it hit me. Was he decorating for Lucy?

"What?" he asked.

"I think she wants to know why we're here," Lucy said, and then poured a cup of coffee and handed it to him. She seemed perfectly comfortable in my kitchen. "Ainsley?"

"Yes, please." I sat down on the barstool that sits under my kitchen island. Odd to have someone else serving coffee in my house. But this whole morning was strange.

She sat a cup in front of me, and then sat down with hers. Greg stayed on the other side of the island rubbing his head.

"Your lead panned out," Lucy said. "How did you find him?"

Wait. What? "Who is he?" Were they talking about the little boy? He'd been on my mind before I slept last night.

"Martin Blakely," Lucy said. "A forensic accountant who used to work for the FBI, that is until he had to go into WITSEC because of death threats."

"Witness protection?" I sipped my coffee. I needed all the caffeine, if I was going to survive this morning.

"Yeah," Greg said. "When you sent me that picture, I

forwarded it on to my contact at the FBI. They knew exactly who he was. He testified for a huge case that involved money launderers in several states. He was the best in his field, and his testimony put a lot of really bad people away about twenty-five years ago."

"But he was an accountant? I don't understand." I had six sips of coffee before I realized I'd forgotten to put cream and Truvia in it.

George barked at the back door, and Greg let him in, and filled up his dog bowl with food.

My dog stared at him.

"Why is he doing that?"

I chuckled. "He gets two Milk Bones on the top, for sleeping through the night."

"But he's never done that before," he said.

I shook my head. "It happened after Shannon and Mike kept him for a few days when I was in the hospital. Now, it's a thing."

Greg put the bones on the top of the food.

And George ate like there was no tomorrow. Food was going all over the floor, but I wasn't worried. He always cleaned up after himself.

"Do you think he was murdered by these guys? And why would he leave WITSEC? That seems like the safest place for him."

"Two months after he went in the program, there was an attempt on his life," Greg said. "They moved him again and he was in Phoenix for about six months, and then he vanished. There had to be some kind of leak for them to find him, but the agents involved never found out who it was.

"He left all of his belongings behind. The FBI and WITSEC hadn't heard from him for over twenty years. They thought he might be dead all this time," Lucy said as she put her coffee down. "As in someone kidnapped him, and then killed him."

"Well, now he is really dead. You didn't answer my other question. Do you think the people he testified against, killed him?"

Greg shook his head. "We're investigating all possibilities. There was unidentified DNA on the back of his Santa suit. Unfortunately, it could belong to anyone. There hasn't been a match, yet. We're still running it through the database."

"Kids are always hugging on Santa. That might be one reason why you can't find a match. But what about the handprints on his back?"

"Davy, I mean, Martin was a large man. But the heels of the hands on his back are small, like a woman's. There's no way, though, someone that size would be able to push the victim hard enough to hurt him," Greg said. "Do you have anything to eat? I'm hungry."

"Greg!" Lucy said.

"She's my sister," he said. "And I wasn't going to make her cook."

Before I could answer him, he pulled out eggs and bacon and started throwing breakfast together.

"This is all very interesting, but why did you feel the need to deliver the news this early?"

Lucy grinned as she watched Greg cook. I'm not sure she was honest about her feelings the other night. She had that look of a woman who was interested.

Ugh, I couldn't imagine why—he's gross. I mean, handsome in his way, but gross.

It took all my wits not to sneer at the idea of them dating and then an errant thought slapped the side of my head.

"Wait a minute. You decorated your house?"

"It is Christmas, Ains."

I snorted. "Yes, but you never put anything up because you're always working."

"I do the outside lights every year." He grunted. And I knew I'd hit a nerve. I looked at him and then Lucy, who had tucked her head so I couldn't read her expression. Was it because she'd stayed with him?

"We found your friend Caroline," Greg said, effectively changing the subject. "We also need the photos Don gave you for verification on Martin. The FBI sent some shots of him that they had."

"Where was she?"

"In a drunk tank in San Antonio. Seems she and Mary Beth, the other woman you told us about, went on a bender on the River Walk. They're going in front of a judge for drunk and disorderly this morning."

San Antonio was only an hours' drive away and had amazing bars. But this was hard to believe. "No way. They're not like that."

He stepped back slightly. "I always tell you that you never really know people, Ains. You just met those women. For all we know, they could have found out they were seeing the same man, and gone into a jealous rage."

"Yeah. Nah. They seemed cool with one another. I even

saw them hugging each other on the video feed the day after the murder."

Greg and Lucy's heads snapped to look at me.

"Do you remember what time?" she asked. "I don't remember seeing that."

"Well, we were only reviewing around the time of the murder, and just after." Greg put some eggs on plates. Then he set the skillet down in the sink, and pulled the bacon out of the microwave.

"I can't remember exactly. It was before the festival opened on Saturday. I'd been looking for your Christmas thief, who I might have seen by the way. But I'm looking into it."

Or Jeff and Lily were. I needed to check in with those two later.

"One woman may not have been able to push him," Lucy said, "but two could."

"I don't think they did it," I said. "What if someone at the festival recognized the victim? When we were at the warehouse, you told me that a lot of that stuff was from a case that was nationwide. That means organized crime, right? Well, we have seventy-five different booths from all over the U.S. and it could be a person who is keeping a low profile."

Greg munched on bacon, and Lucy stared down at her plate.

We were missing something, I just didn't know what.

His phone rang. "Yeah. Huh. Okay. Thanks."

He rubbed his forehead again. "We have another strong suspect."

"Who is it?"

My brother's blue eyes drilled into mine.

Me?

"That guy you went out with the other night."

"Oh. I thought we already had him down as one."

"We did, but he has a rap sheet."

"What did he do?"

"It doesn't matter." Greg's eyes narrowed. "We'll be looking at him and maybe you shouldn't date him."

I rolled my eyes. "I kind of have a coffee date with him."

"Ainsley." My brother sighed dramatically.

Lucy snorted and then covered her face. I was beginning to really like her.

"It's just coffee and it's in a public place that my best friend owns. I think I'll be okay. Besides, he's more likely to talk to me. And you said the hands that pushed him were a woman's. He's tall and has manly hands."

"We can't know that for sure," Greg said. "What time are you meeting him?"

"Ten-ish."

Greg frowned.

"You've got to be in court," Lucy said. "I'll cover her."

"Thanks," Greg said.

"Sitting right here, people. I can take care of myself."

"We should head out," he said. Then he proceeded to scoop an entire egg into his mouth.

"Photos?" Lucy asked.

I pointed to the coffee table.

She scooped them up. "See ya later."

I locked the door behind them and turned to find George staring at me with a perplexed look on his face.

"I know. I know. They annoy me, too. I guess we better get ready."

I TRIED TO follow my gut, which said Rob was not guilty. He had opportunity but as far as I could see, he didn't have motive.

Before heading to the coffee shop, I parked behind where their trailers were. I was about to walk around one of the big RVs when I heard someone fighting.

I peeked around the corner to find Rob and Anika going at it. She was pointing a finger at him and yelling.

"You're not going to ruin this for us," she said. "I don't know why you're being so mean to everyone, but you need to get a grip. We're at the end. Don't let everyone go home with a bad attitude because you're worried about whatever it is you won't tell us about."

Rob tugged on his beard. "I'm not mean. What, are we in high school now? If people can't take criticism, they need to grow up."

Anika's hands went to her hips and she took a deep breath.

"You need to tell me what's wrong. Whatever it is, it's eating you up inside."

Rob shook his head. "It's not a big deal. I've got the message. Don't yell at Brewer for getting drunk and missing his shift. I'm tired okay? I worked sixteen hours straight yesterday. And now I have to go have coffee with the sheriff's nosy sister, who probably just wants more info about Davy."

Oh. Well. Maybe he was a murderer. I turned back around and drove away a few seconds later.

Maybe, he was just tired. I wasn't always the best the day after a long day. But that conversation had shown me a different side of Rob. And it sounded as if he'd been cranky with everyone.

What was he upset about?

At ten, I sat down at a table by the window with my dirty chai, and a couple of cream cheese kolaches, and a sausage roll.

Lucy was as the next table with her laptop. It was uncomfortable having her look over my shoulder but I wasn't really given a choice.

Nerves buzzed around my belly. Rob had hurt my feelings. I could admit that. Calling me nosy, even if it's true, was mean.

A few minutes later, Rob ordered at the register, and then turned to wave at me. He did look really tired. After he picked up his coffee and pastry, he sat down across from me.

"How are you?" he asked. "The festival seems to be going well."

"Fine." My voice was a bit sharp. "You look tired."

He sighed. "It was a long night. And I seem to be in a foul mood lately. I'm not sure why."

Maybe, because you accidentally killed Davy? Even if he had called me nosy, I couldn't see him killing someone on purpose.

"Happens to the best of us."

Have I mentioned I kind of suck at small talk?

"The other night didn't end great." He took a sip of his

coffee. "I wasn't sure you'd show up this morning."

"It wasn't your fault. Our fire department doesn't get a lot of action."

Today he wore a baseball cap on backward, which usually annoyed me. But it worked on him. And he was in a vintage Def Leppard T-shirt and jeans.

Anika hadn't lied about his uniform of choice.

"That fire chief, Jake, was pretty cool. We chatted after you left. We play a lot of the same video games. And I know what you said, but I'm pretty sure he's into you."

No way I'd touch that one. Jake and I definitely had to talk about things. But that was a convo for another day. I'd decided to get through my busiest season and then I'd just talk to Jake like a grown-up to see where his head was at.

"I didn't know he played video games. What kind of stuff do you play?"

"It sounds childish, right? Most women think so—at least the ones who don't play. I'm kind of old school. I like Modern Warfare and Warcraft. Though, I play a lot of different games. When we're traveling, it's a fun thing to do with the guys and Anika. She's the best one out of all of us. I guess it's my stress relief, even though we don't have that much since we love what we do."

"I read a lot."

He leaned forward on his elbows. "That makes sense. You're a teacher or a professor, right? Do you make the kids call you Dr. McGregor?"

I shook my head. "I'm not into titles. They do call me professor, sometimes." Acutely aware that Lucy listened to every word, I tried to keep our conversation from anything too incendiary. "How old were you when you started playing video games?" For some reason, my brain had trouble coming up with small talk sometimes. Especially when I was nervous.

He grimaced. "I wasn't a great kid," he said. "I tended to get into trouble a lot. My mom and grandmother tried their best. When I was around fifteen, I was grounded for a month. And I ended up playing a bunch of different games then."

"I can't imagine you being a troublemaker."

He chuckled. "My mom and grandma were ready to ship me off to military school."

"Really?"

He nodded. "My dad wasn't a great guy, and I got in with a bad crowd in my late teens. I never stole or hurt anyone. But I did go joyriding. I love things that go fast. I think that's part of my fascination with the carnival. Anyway, I'm lucky those records are sealed.

"And then when I was eighteen, I hacked the local FBI offices. I was lucky I didn't end up in jail. But it gave me a record. In a strange way, it helped me get my first job creating apps. And I've been following the straight and narrow ever since."

That explained his rap sheet. "Until you ran away with the carnival."

He laughed. "I guess that's my way of being subversive these days. How about you? How did you end up in Sweet River?"

I told him about living in Chicago, but left out the muggings.

"I love it here." I took a sip of my coffee. "The people are amazing and it's been a wonderful place to follow my dreams."

He sat back and crossed his arms. "We've had a lot of fun here. Well, except for what happened to Davy. Have you heard anything else?"

I shook my head. "Not really anything that wasn't in the papers. You said you'd met him last year?"

"Yep. We did Arlington, Dallas, and I think Round Top with him and Caroline last year. It all runs together after a while. I'm going to miss him. He always made me laugh and he had the best stories about characters around the world. I'm sorry he wasn't a writer because it would be great to read about his travels."

Davy had been in Texas for at least a year if he'd hit all of those spots.

"I thought you didn't know him that well?"

"Are you going to cross-examine me?" He tensed.

I laughed, but it came out as more of a squeak. "No. I just remembered you said you didn't know much about him."

He frowned. "I don't. We hung out. Maybe had a beer or five. But he never talked about himself. His stories were always about other people."

"I've heard that a lot."

"Can I ask you something?" He seemed to relax a bit, but his eyes were fixated over my shoulder. Crud. Had he recognized Lucy?

"Was Davy murdered?"

"Are you pumping me for information?"

"You seem to be the only one around here who knows anything."

"Like I said, not so much."

"Do you think the police will want to question me?" The only sign he might be nervous was the tapping of his finger on the table.

"I have no idea. Did you do something that would make them want to?"

His head jerked back with surprise. "What motive would I have to hurt him?"

"As far as I can see, you don't have one."

He stood and loomed over me. "I need to get going." His hands were in fists.

A chair behind me scraped against the wooden floor.

Lucy stood beside our table. She flashed her badge.

He looked from her to me, and his eyebrows drew together.

I don't blame you, dude. I'd be mad at me, too.

"I heard you talking about the victim. Would you mind coming down to the station for a chat?" she asked Rob.

"Did you set me up?" he said through his teeth.

"I had nothing to do with this. I swear."

When I glanced up I found him staring at me. He was definitely angry.

"She didn't," Lucy said. "Like I said, I happened to overhear. Will you come with me?"

He nodded. Then he stood and followed her through the shop.

"Wait. Do you still want to go to a party with me Saturday night?" I blurted out. I don't know why. I just felt horribly guilty even though none of this was my fault. I blamed my overprotective brother.

He and Lucy turned and stared at me. I might as well have asked him if he had a pet dragon.

"Sorry. Not the right time."

His eyebrow went up, and they turned toward the door.

"Wow. That might be a new low," Shannon said from beside me. What was it with people and their ninja moves? "You get him arrested and then ask him out. I'm beginning to believe you are into guys who aren't available emotionally and literally."

I smirked. "Funny. I don't know why I did that." The whole time we'd been talking, it felt like Rob was leaving something big out of his story.

How did he go from hacking to graduating from SMU? Something must have happened. And was that really all he'd done?

My phone beeped. It was a text from Lily.
We found the bike.

Chapter Seventeen

A FEW HOURS later, I was at the shop. I'd been forbidden to go down to the station while they questioned Rob. And, because my brother can be an obstinate jerk, he refused to tell me why they suspected him. Other than he was the last one seen going into the Santa house.

I couldn't concentrate on the paperwork in front of me and was about to head up to the registers, when there was a knock on the office door. I only shut it when I was trying to focus on numbers, but no one ever knocked around here.

I stood and opened it. "Hey," Jeff said. He and Lily both wore those funny reindeer-horn headbands.

"Did you buy those from Don's booth?"

They nodded. "And I picked up Christmas presents for my family." Lily held up a bag.

"But that's not why we're here," Jeff added. "School is out in about an hour and a half, and we can follow the kid on the bike."

George stood and stretched in the corner. "Why don't we take a walk first. You can leave your bag in here, Lily, and I'll lock the door."

We headed out down the path that ran along the river, behind the festival booths. It was cloudy, and I smelled rain in the air. George clomped along. "Where did you find the bike?"

"At the elementary school, which means he's definitely under twelve years old," Lily said. "One of the teachers came out and was looking at us like she was ready to call the cops, but I took a pic and it definitely matches the one you showed us in the video."

I actually felt sorry for the kid. If he was that young and stealing, it probably meant his family was struggling. Still, it was wrong and his parents needed to know.

"You guys don't have to come with me," I said. "I don't want to risk getting you in trouble."

The pair laughed. "We knew you'd say that," Jeff said. "If you don't let us come with you, we'll just tail you."

As we made our way to the other end of the park, we passed the carnival. Rob was there talking to Rick this time. Rick waved at me. Rob turned to see who it was, and gave me a nod. His sunglasses blocked his eyes, but I'm sure he wasn't happy with me.

"Hurry up, George."

After George did his business, we headed back to the shop. I left George at the front of the store where Mrs. Whedon and Maria were running the registers.

"I have to run an errand. Do you mind keeping an eye on George?"

Maria smiled. "Of course I don't mind," she said.

Mrs. Whedon pointed at George. "No slobbering."

I swear he grinned at her. She might have been grumpy, but my dog knows a good soul when he sees one. She rubbed him behind the ears.

"I won't be long."

A few minutes later, I parked on the street in front of the school near the bike racks at the elementary. It did feel wrong to be tailing a kid. But beyond the stolen items, we needed to make sure he was okay. Lily's comment about him possibly being on his own broke my heart.

Most of the kids had gone, but the bike was still there. And then, a small boy, who couldn't have been more than a second grader, came out. He unlocked the bike and climbed on.

That's when I realized we were very conspicuous in my SUV. I let him take off, and then followed slowly behind. Just about mile out, he stopped at Mr. Green's general store.

"You guys stay in here. I'm going inside."

I followed him in and picked up a big bag of sour cream and onion chips, and three waters.

The kid bought a half gallon of milk, peanut butter, and bread.

Mr. Green leaned over and ruffled the boy's hair. "How are you doing today, son?"

The boy smiled at him. "I'm good, Mr. Green. Mom asked me to stop on the way home from school."

"Tell her I don't mind delivering to her. Is she feeling any better?"

The boy frowned and shook his head.

Mr. Green's brow furrowed. "I see. You let me know if you two need anything. And be careful riding home. I worry about you being alone on these roads."

"I'm a big kid," the boy said. "I'll be okay."

The mom was sick and this little guy was taking care of them. My nose was suddenly quite sniffly.

I had my money ready, so I could check out quickly.

"Hi, Ainsley."

"Hey, Mr. Green, you ready for the holidays?"

He laughed. "Do I have a choice in this town?"

"You make a good point. That little boy who was in here, is his mom sick? He seems awful small to be running around on his own."

The older man frowned. "He is way too young. I worry about him. But I didn't report it to social services because I know his poor mom is doing her best. And he's a great kid."

Who steals. But the reason why was becoming more apparent.

"I just overheard you guys and it sounded like a sad story."

He nodded.

"Well, I better get going." I handed him the money and hurried out to my car.

"I thought you were never coming back out," Lily said.

"Jeff is jogging behind him to keep track. They went down that way." She pointed down the road that led to another set of campgrounds on the other side of the lake.

It wasn't long before we saw Jeff. I pulled over to the side of the road and he hopped in. The little boy wasn't far ahead.

"You must have been running pretty fast," I said.

Jeff took a few seconds to answer as he caught his breath. "For a kid, he pedals fast."

About a half mile later, the boy rode his bike down a side road to one of the campgrounds. We drove through trees that then opened up to a meadow. There was only one small camper and an old truck.

We stayed back, as he climbed off his bike. And then flipped an outside switch on the camper. A magical fairyland opened up before us. Lights and tinsel strung in the trees. The small animatronic Santa waving hello on a table under the awning. There were pots of poinsettias all around in a colorful display. And several small Christmas trees with lights and ragtag ornaments.

"Just a heads-up," Lily said, "I might cry. Do you think he did all of this himself?"

I nodded, not trusting my voice. He grabbed his backpack and the groceries and went to the door of the camper.

"What do we do?" Jeff asked.

"We have to knock on the door." Even though I didn't want to. I didn't want to be the awful person who told his mom that he'd stolen everything.

And then I remembered seeing him in the video with Davy/Martin.

"I know what to do."

The kids followed me to the front door of the camper where I knocked. The door opened and a woman in her late twenties with dark brown hair, wearing unicorn pajamas answered the door. I liked her instantly.

She was beautiful in a waif kind of way, except her skin had an odd gray color, and there were extremely dark circles under her eyes. She was suffering and my heart hurt for her.

"Hi," she said, as she gave us a wary look. "Can I help you?" The little boy came up behind her. He was a blond cherub with the sweetest face.

I cleared my throat. "Hi, I'm Ainsley McGregor. My

brother is the sheriff of Sweet River." When I mentioned my brother, the little boy's eyes nearly bugged out his head.

"Is there something wrong?"

I forced myself to smile. "Oh, no. I just needed to ask your son a few questions. My brother has asked me to look into a case he's working on."

"And you want to talk to Terry?" She glanced down at her son, and put a loving hand on his head.

"If it's okay with you. I promise we won't take much of your time." There was no way I was telling this poor woman about what her son had been doing. She had enough to deal with. But now I was into it.

"Sure. Why don't you come in?"

The camper was tidy and smelled of cloves and cinnamon. We sat down at the small banquette across from her and the boy.

"Hi, Terry, I'm Ainsley. I run the store in town called Bless Your Art, but I sometimes assist my brother Greg, the sheriff, with his cases."

Okay, that was a stretch but I was working on this one.

Terry blinked and a tear rolled down his cheek. "I'm sorry. I know it was bad."

My heart twisted in my chest hard. I couldn't breathe.

"I'm not here about that. I promise."

"About what?" his mother asked.

"I borrowed stuff without asking. I was gonna take it back after Christmas. But I wanted to make things pretty for you because you've been sad."

"Baby, what are you talking about?"

"The decorations outside. People weren't throwing them

in the trash. I borrowed them."

His mom wiped the tears from his cheeks with her thumbs. "Little Boo, you know that's stealing. It's one thing to ask to borrow things. Or to take things that you see on the side of the road. What you did was stealing."

He cried hard then. "I'm sorry, Momma."

My eyes welled up, and I swallowed hard.

"I know you are. You're my good boy. But I need you to promise that you'll never take things again. You have to ask permission or buy them."

He nodded. "I felt bad in my heart."

She gave him a kiss on the top of his head. "I'm sure you did. That feeling means you've done something really wrong. In the future, you don't want to ever feel it again. Right?"

"Yes, ma'am."

"We'll take everything back."

He nodded.

I cleared my throat again. Unshed tears stuck in the back of it. "While we were aware it was Terry, that isn't really why I'm here," I said. Okay, it was.

"Oh. No. What now?" the mom asked.

"Terry, do you remember when you met Santa in town? He gave you candy canes."

"Wait, you went into town? Terry. School and then home. You know the rules. And you never talk to strangers or take candy from them."

"Yes, ma'am, but he was Santa."

I wasn't sure if he said it to me or her.

"Can you tell me what Santa said to you that day?"

He scrunched up his face. "I think he knew I was bad."

"Why is that?"

"He said, 'You must always choose to do the right thing even when it's hard.' Then he gave me the candy canes."

The hard choices comment made me wonder if he'd been talking about his speaking out against the bad guys in the case he'd been involved in.

His mother closed her eyes and took a deep breath. "I'm not sure if I'm more upset that you went into town by yourself or that you took candy from a stranger."

"Did he say anything else to you?"

"Just for me to be a good boy. I don't want to be a bad kid, Momma. I just wanted to do somethin' nice for you."

The mom sighed. "I know, honey. But taking from others is always wrong. Promise me, this won't ever happen again."

His little face was covered in tears as he nodded.

"Will there be charges pressed against him?" she asked.

"No." At least, I hoped not. "We were more interested in what Santa said to him." I glanced back at Jeff, who was texting furiously on his phone. He'd stayed close to the door, as the small camper was already crowded with all of us inside.

I wonder what that was about?

Lily was doing the same thing under the table.

"Hey, gang, can you take Terry outside with you? I mean, if that's okay with you?"

His mom nodded.

Terry and Lily headed outside, as Jeff held the door.

"Ma'am, may I ask a personal question about your illness? I promise it's for a good reason," Jeff said.

"Jeff?" I asked.

"Uh, my dad is a doctor in Austin. Actually, a surgeon. I texted him about you. And he wanted to know who you've been seeing and the diagnosis."

"Jeff, that's very personal." I turned to give him my evil teacher eye.

"I know. But I'm just trying to help. I sent your picture to my dad, and he's worried about you."

Oh. My. This kid.

"I'm sorry," I said to her. "He doesn't always understand boundaries. You don't have to say anything."

"I. Um." She had that deer-in-the-headlights fright in her eyes. She stood shakily and went to look out her kitchen window. "I had no idea Terry was—I don't want to lose him." She sniffed.

"Jeff. Why don't you join Lily and shut the door?"

For once, he did what I asked and shut the door behind him.

"No one is going to take that little boy away from you." It was a promise I wasn't sure I could keep but I would die trying. "Let us help you. Tell me what's been going on. That way we can figure out the next steps."

She rubbed her head and frowned. A bunch of strangers intruding on her life had to be stressful, but I didn't want her to feel like she was alone. I had this extreme need to make sure she and Terry were taken care of.

"I was working in Dallas and things were great. And then I got this terrible virus. It attacked my lungs and my kidneys and I can't seem to shake it. I lost my job, and my health care. I sold everything, bought this little camper and we moved here last August.

"I'd read about Sweet River in a travel magazine and it was pretty. I was doing better for a while, but then...I don't have the money for a doctor. So, while I appreciate the offer. There's nothing you can do. But I promise I'll look after my son better. I'll take him back and forth to school. You don't have to worry." She looked like she was about to collapse.

"I'm not worried. I can tell you are a great mom. But it's okay to ask for help sometimes. I had to do the same thing a few months ago when I landed in the hospital. And you're in the right place. In Sweet River, we take care of our own."

There was a knock on the door.

"Come in," she said.

Jeff held out his phone to her. "I'm sorry. My dad really wants to talk to you. He's genuinely worried."

She sank back into the seat of the banquette, and seemed to fold in on herself.

"I'm sorry. But I don't know you people. I think it might be best if you go."

We were pushing her too hard and she wasn't well. But it didn't look like time was on her side.

"Why don't you talk to the doctor first? It's free. It's just a phone call. Jeff shouldn't have been so pushy, but I can promise you his heart is in the right place."

After taking the phone, she closed her eyes as if trying to regain her strength. "Hello." She sat there and listened for a couple of minutes. "Yes. For the past year. Are you sure?" There was relief there, as if the burden she'd been carrying had lifted. "No, I don't have insurance. Oh. But... Well, thank you. I need to find someone to help with my son, first."

She handed the phone back to Jeff. He put it to his ear. "Yes, sir," he said, and then walked back outside.

"He wants me and Terry to come to Austin tonight. He thinks he can cure me. I'm sort of amazed he knew what was wrong just by seeing a picture of me. He must be a very good doctor. He said he usually treats sports injuries, but that he came across someone who had the same sort of symptoms I did when he was working in an ER years ago. I feel like you guys are fairy godmothers."

I hadn't even known his dad was a surgeon, but I nodded.

"I realize we just met, but do you need me to watch Terry? I don't mind at all." I knew nothing about taking care of children but I was sure I could figure it out.

She shook her head. "How well do you know these kids who are with you?"

"They are students of mine. I teach part-time at the college. But they are awesome human beings. Why?"

"Between the girl's parents and Jeff's, they have it all sorted. Terry is going to stay with her parents and little brother, while I'm going through the tests. It's…too much. I worry about Terry. He's been through so much, and you just told me he's been stealing."

She sighed heavily.

My heart hurt for her but this was a great opportunity.

"Why don't you meet everyone involved? It won't hurt to go to Austin and get checked out by the doctors. Then you can make an informed decision. And I have a feeling this is your Christmas miracle. I don't normally believe in that sort of stuff, but it's kind of cool that you had just the right people here at the right time. If it were me, I'd take advantage of the opportunity."

"My brain hurts from all the kindness," she said. "They don't even know me."

"Well, if the parents are anything like their kids, they're great people. And I'll be following up with everyone. You don't need to worry about anything but getting healthy."

"What about the sheriff? What my son did was wrong."

"I'll take care of it. There were extenuating circumstances."

Greg wouldn't be happy with me about this.

But the relief on her face was worth it.

"Now, let's get you ready to travel."

Chapter Eighteen

IT FELT LIKE one of those days that had been several days long. I needed a hot shower, my softest pajamas, and maybe some holiday movies to cheer me up. Terry and his mom would be taken care of and I'd already contacted the store owners. And in true Sweet River fashion, they all wanted to know what they could do for the family.

My brother was oddly silent when I called him and told him everything. All he said was, "Are you sure they're going to be okay?" It was very un-Greg like.

I'd expected him to yell for butting in. I'd done exactly what he'd asked me not to do. But he didn't.

I wasn't disappointed.

As I pulled up in the drive, there was someone on my porch.

"This is turning into a regular thing," I said to George. But it wasn't Lucy this time. "What happened to people letting you know before they just showed up? And how did he know where I live?"

With all the drama of the last few hours, I'd totally forgotten what had happened early this morning with Rob. He hadn't been happy with me. I blew out a breath and wondered if I should text my brother.

"You'll protect me. Right, George?"

"RURruuh," he said.

I took that as an affirmative.

"Hi, what brings you out here tonight?"

Rob leaned forward on the porch railings. "I thought maybe I should let you know I'm not a murderer or a serial killer. Or any of the other bad things you might be thinking."

I nodded. "You have my number—you could have called."

He frowned. "Oh. I just thought it was a conversation that would be better face-to-face. And I was exhausted earlier today. I haven't been sleeping great, then I piled a sixteen-hour day on top of that, and then I got hauled off to the police station."

No way I'd apologize. It wasn't my fault.

It was uncomfortable as we stood there looking at one another. I didn't like guys I didn't know well showing up at my house. It felt...stalkery.

"I can leave, if you want. It just dawned on me that this might look bad. I swear it was more about talking to you face-to-face."

"I'm curious how you found out where I live." While it wasn't exactly a secret, I was usually careful about giving out my personal information to strangers.

"I dropped the video game *Lords of War* off at Jake's the other day," he said. "I saw you drive past his place and I was curious. When I left, I drove down the road and I saw your car. And as I say it, I realize just how creepy all this sounds. I'll leave. I'm sorry, Ainsley. It's been a rough day and I haven't been thinking straight."

He walked down the steps toward a big, silver pickup truck.

I sighed, not for the first time that day. "It's okay. Why don't you come out to the backyard, and I'll get us something to drink? George needs to do his run before dinner."

I wasn't super comfortable having a stranger in the house. I'd done that before, maybe a couple of times, and it hadn't worked well for me.

I opened the back gate, and George dashed through. His friend Mr. Squirrel, the bane of my existence, sat on the top of the back fence. The furry rat took one look at George, and ran for the line of trees on the back end of my property.

"Well, that has to be disappointing." Rob laughed as he sat down on one of the lounge chairs on my back deck.

"It's a game they like to play. Would you like a beer, water, or I may have wine?"

"Water's good," he said. "My head is messed up enough, even though I finally took a two-hour nap."

I unlocked the back door. Dumped my stuff on the kitchen counter, and poured filtered water out of the fridge. Well water is not always the tastiest, but with the filter, it wasn't awful.

Making sure I had my brother's number queued up, I stuck my phone in the pocket of my sweater. One can never be too careful.

"Here you go?" I handed him the drink, and then sat mine down on the table between the two chairs. "I'm going to grab his bowls. I'll be right back."

I filled his food bowl up and the water, and set them on the right side of the door. He'd eat when he was ready.

"Right. I'm sorry about what happened this morning," I said, even though he didn't seem to be angry.

"It's not your fault. The investigator explained she'd really just overheard us and wanted to see if I had relevant info for their case. I should have come forward right after he died. And it wasn't that bad even though it took a couple of hours."

"What happened?"

"I told them the truth."

It wasn't my business but…

"I don't have a right to ask, but I'd like to hear the truth from you."

"I didn't kill Martin, but I did know who he was. I've known for a year. But I wasn't about to tell his secret. It wasn't mine to tell."

"Maybe start from the beginning."

He turned to face me. "Martin was the guy who helped put away my dad," he said. "I mean, if it weren't for him— My mom was trying to divorce my dad when he was arrested for money-laundering.

"Dad had been a legit businessman when my mom married him. But the economy took a downturn and he got in with the wrong people. I remember thinking about him as two people. One day he was this loving guy who liked to take me fishing and then he was an angry jerk who screamed at my mom all the time.

"Right before he was arrested, she found out what his real business was. I was, like, seven, and I remember the argument, even though I didn't know what it was about. She kicked him out of the house. I can't believe he actually left.

"And then she packed up our clothes, and my toys, and we went to my grandma's house. She filed for divorce, but he wasn't having it. He'd have his men show up at my grandma's house and try to harass them. Never touched them, but they'd bang on the doors and shout from the driveway. I remember her stuffing me into a closet and telling me to be very quiet. It was a scary time.

"Then one day, it all stopped. Some suits came to the house and offered her WITSEC protection if she testified against him, but she wouldn't do it. My grandma sold her house, and she and my mom found a way to get us legitimate documents to change our names without my dad finding out."

"Wow." That was a pretty crazy story.

"I know. It's like something out of a movie. But the legal documents are there to back it up."

"Oh, I believe you, it's just I would have never expected a story like that from you."

"I hadn't thought about any of that for years. We moved to Dallas, and had a whole different life there. Except for getting into trouble in my teens, I'd lived a pretty simple life. It sounds awful, and maybe it was the trauma, but I forgot about my dad and all of that. When people asked if I had a dad, I said he died. And I guess I started to believe it."

I could understand that. Kids were good at shoving stuff they didn't want to think about down.

"There's a video of you going into the Santa house, not long before he was killed."

He nodded. "Like I said, I'd known him since we met in Arlington last year. I look a lot like my dad. I have a feeling that Martin had an idea who I was from the first time we met.

"One night, we had a few too many drinks at the campsite and I told him the whole story. And he admitted who he was."

"After keeping that secret for so long?"

"It's crazy. I get it. But it's the truth. We were kind of in the same boat, trying to stay out of sight. No way would I snitch, and I knew he wouldn't either. Since Dad died in prison five years ago—we thought we were both safe."

"You would think," I said softly. If his story hadn't checked out, there was no way my brother would have let him go. "Do you think someone from your dad's past killed Martin?"

"It's a possibility but I don't know how they would have found him. He was still very careful. And it has been a long time. Most of those guys are dead or in prison still."

George was running in circles, which meant he was about ready to settle down. "I'm curious why you felt like you had to come out here tonight."

"Anika says I've been grumpy, lately. I don't even remember what I said at the coffee shop today. Have I mentioned the not sleeping? It's not an excuse. But I wanted to apologize if I said anything that hurt your feelings."

You did, but I can't tell you how I heard it. "No worries."

"You're into Jake. I could tell the other night by the way you two kept looking at each other, but I'm still grateful you let us do this event. And we'd like to come back next year.

"The people are nice—and we've never pulled in this kind of revenue in one week. I just didn't want—I was worried my past might make you think twice about having us back. And I don't want to do that to my crew. Seemed like it was best to be truthful."

I understood his logic. "Don't worry. I already had the committee draw up the contracts for you guys to come back next year."

"Really?" He seemed genuinely pleased.

I nodded. "You're wrong about Jake and me. We're just friends."

"Does he know that? He seems awful protective for a friend. He kept talking about how amazing you are when I went to his house."

I laughed. "He did?"

"I don't want to horn in on a relationship, but I'm still game for that party if you want me to go. You're a catch. Of course, we'd be going just as friends. I understand that. But maybe we could make your *friend*, Jake, jealous as a bonus."

I snorted. I'm not sure men ever saw me as anything other than a friend. "Thanks for saying I'm a catch. And yes, going to the party with you would be fun. I don't play games, though. If Jake gets jealous, well, that's his problem."

He shook his head. "I just hope he doesn't punch my face."

I howled with laughter. "He's not really a violent dude," I said. "He might write you up for a fire code, but that would be the extent of it."

We sat there as George began to wind down.

"There is one thing I forgot to tell your brother and that other cop. I just thought of it while we were talking."

"What's that?"

"I mentioned Martin was thinner than he'd been a year ago, and he seemed confused. It took him a minute to remember who I was. He was always sharp. And he was sweating—even though it was cool outside.

"But with all that padding and that velvet suit, it made sense at the time. I asked him if he was all right, and he told me yes. He was munching on a couple of candy canes. I thought that was weird. Why did he have more than one? We talked about meeting up for lunch when he had his break the next day. Then he told me about pulling Rudolph's tail, and I walked out the back door."

I chewed on my lip. "Did it close? The door?"

"I don't remember it shutting behind me. I thought it was cool that it slid open like one of those doors on *Star Trek*."

Anyone could have come through that back panel. Next year, I'd make sure we had security cameras behind the booths as well. Though, I hoped nothing like this ever happened again.

"Aren't you worried about someone trying to hurt you?"

He shook his head. "Your brother said we're safe. The FBI is staking out our caravan. I've got to go tell all of my friends about that. They're going to freak out."

I chuckled. "You're probably right about that. But you guys are tight. I wouldn't worry too much. Knowing them, they'll probably think it's cool."

"We'll see. I'm not sure where the party is. Do you want me to pick you up here?"

"There's no reason for you to drive all the way out here, since it's in town. Her place is right above the coffee shop where we were today." If the weather held out, the white elephant party would be at Shannon's rooftop garden above her shop. It was one of my favorite places in town. "I'll meet you there."

He waved goodbye, and a minute later a truck engine started up.

My mind whirled with all the information. How crazy was it that something from so long ago, and thousands of miles away, had touched our little town? It only showed how small the world really was.

George stopped running and stared toward the forest behind the house. He growled.

It was probably just an animal.

I shivered. But you could never be too sure. Hunters and teens hung out in the woods, even though it was considered private property. The tiny hairs on my neck pricked up.

"George. Treat."

He didn't come in like normal. "George. Please."

There must have been something because he started walking backward toward me. It would have been funny if his growl wasn't growing more menacing. Whatever was out there, George didn't like it, and he was a pretty good judge of character.

I opened the door and shook the box of Milk Bones and that finally turned his attention to me.

He ran inside. I slammed, and then locked, the door. Then I ran to the front to double-check that lock. George groaned.

Crud. I'd left his food out on the deck.

The motion sensors on the back fence would go off if

anything came too near.

"Sit." I pointed at him. Then, I opened the door and grabbed his food and water bowls, and slammed it again.

My nerves jangled and my hand shook as I put the bowls down.

Stop it. Why would anyone be after me?

I did just have a felon's son at my house.

It was just an animal. Stop being so paranoid.

Just the same, I set the alarm, and turned all of the lights on.

Then I prayed I didn't have any late-night visitors. I wasn't sure my nerves could take it.

Chapter Nineteen

I HAD SATURDAY afternoon off. I'd planned to shop at the festival, take a nap, and then get ready for the party. Even though the store was crowded, I didn't feel guilty. Just about everyone with a booth was working, and I had three people at the registers. Two to run them, and one to package. We had a great team.

It was the holiday parade tonight. That was why Shannon planned the party to happen on her apartment's rooftop, so we'd have a front-row seat. All sorts of holiday celebrations were represented during the parade, from Hanukkah to Kwanzaa, and it was a highlight of the whole season.

But first—shopping. I'd picked Maria as my Secret Santa person. I couldn't decide if I wanted to get something Christmassy for her, or a gift that was more personal. As the mom of five kids, she didn't get a lot of time for herself. And she loved shiny things as much as I did.

The booth where I'd told Mike to find the peacock things had jewelry she'd love.

As I passed by Armand and Justin's booth, they were fighting at the back of it. I'd wanted to stop by to see if they'd sell more on consignment, but now didn't seem like the right time.

I wonder what that was all about?

"Ainsley?" I turned to find Mary Beth waving at me from her booth. She hadn't been around Thursday or Friday, probably still sleeping off her hangover.

Her checkered past made me wonder why my brother didn't consider her more of a suspect. But when I'd asked him about it, he said her alibi was solid. When I brought up all the dead husbands, he said that marrying older men wasn't a crime. The youngest one had been eighty-three and they all died of natural causes.

"How are you?"

She shook her head. "Been better. I think I might have picked up a bug in jail the other night."

I took a step back.

"That's probably a good idea. I've been coughing the last two days. At least the weather's warm, but I think I want to head home tonight."

"Oh? We'll miss you."

Her lips twitched. "I'm too old to be working while I'm ill, but I was wondering if I could give you some of the quilts to sell on consignment? You don't have to give me any money upfront. Maybe you could just send me a check after the holidays?"

Her quilts were gorgeous and quite different in style from the ones we sold in the store.

"Are you sure? I don't mind putting money in your pocket."

She shook her head. "I trust you. I just hate to lose out on sales because I need to go home and rest."

"We have volunteers who can help run your booth, if you wanted to keep it open. We always have about twenty people, in case someone has an emergency or isn't feeling well. You could go back to your camper and rest."

It was usually for a few hours, but we could make an exception. It was obvious she was ill. At least, she was wearing a mask. It was quilted out of green and red fabric with Christmas trees.

"I appreciate that, hon, but I think I'm done. I'm old and it takes me a while to get over things." She started hacking again and I took another step back.

"Okay. I'm happy to take any or all of the quilts. I'll send a volunteer down from the shop. You just need to give me a list of inventory and how much you want to sell them for, and we'll get you sorted."

"That's great. You're such a sweetheart. Thank you."

"No problem. You take care of yourself." I handed her my card. "If you decide you can't wait to the end of today, just text me and I'll send someone down right away."

"You are a blessing, darling. I was wondering if you'd had any more news about Davy? I was out of sorts the last couple of days and haven't heard much. Did they find out who hurt him?"

There wasn't a lot I could tell her. Greg had the local paper hold off running an article—one of the benefits of living in a small town. Only a few people knew who Davy really was, and he wanted to keep it that way.

After what Rob told me, I understood. The whole thing was like something out of a Harlen Coben thriller.

"Um, I've been so busy at the store—I really haven't had a chance to talk to my brother." That was at least true. He had several ongoing investigations. "There was an article in the paper a few days ago. The ME said the case was still under investigation for suspicious circumstances."

She frowned and wrapped her arms around herself. "That's just crazy. No one would want to hurt Davy—he was sweet. I know I keep saying that but he was."

Maybe it was the cold, but her eyes brimmed with tears. As much as I wanted to comfort her, I had no time to catch her cold. I had a lot of people depending on me these days and I had to be extra careful.

"I hope you're right," I said. "Are you going to be okay?"

She pulled the mask down and dabbed her nose with a tissue, and then waved the paper toward me. "I'm fine. Just a silly old woman."

"You are not silly or old. My guess is you need to sit down and rest. Why don't I text the team, and have one of them come down and pack up? You should rest in your camper tonight, and then head out tomorrow after a good night's sleep."

"That's a better plan. Caroline and I went on a bender and I'm just too old for that these days."

"Why did you go to San Antonio? We have bars around here."

"Two silly old women acting younger than they are. She'd never been to the River Walk and I wanted to show her. Caroline's been so sad. And we thought we'd do our own send-off for Davy. I often forget why I don't drink tequila anymore but those margaritas were amazing."

I chuckled. She wasn't wrong about the margaritas. Even though the River Walk was a tourist trap these days, they still had the best drinks.

"Well, I hope you feel better."

"Thank you for everything—I hope to see you again soon."

I waved, and then pulled my phone out of my pocket to text Carrie about picking up the quilts. She was working on inventory and keeping the shelves stocked. I told her to wear a mask and gloves to protect herself from germs.

I turned to head to the booth with the jewelry and found Caroline staring daggers at Mary Beth.

Just keep moving, Ainsley.

But I couldn't stop myself.

"Everything going okay?"

"Fine," she said, her mouth set in a grim line. Gone was the sweet woman from last weekend.

"Is there anything you need?"

She shook her head, never taking her eyes off of Mary Beth.

"Are you angry with her?"

She pulled her angry gaze toward me, and I was quite sorry I'd asked.

"I can't see how that's your business one way or the other."

Okay then.

"Have a nice day." I waved.

Something was going on between those two. They'd cared for the same man and ended up in the drunk tank. You'd think that would create a bonding experience. Whatever it was, I didn't have time to be nosy today. I had things to do.

After buying gifts for Maria, Shannon, and my brother—

and a few dozen things for myself—I headed back to my car and dumped my bags.

Then I hit my head on the hatch coming down.

Did I mention how brilliant I am sometimes? I winced. I'd been distracted by Caroline and Mary Beth, and I felt like I'd forgotten something. I pulled the list out of my pocket.

Oh. No. I hadn't picked up a white elephant gift. And I probably needed to get one for Rob. He might not know he was supposed to bring one.

Since Armand and Justin had ornaments, and their booth wasn't very far down, I headed that way.

They assisted customers and seemed to be over their argument.

"Hello, gorgeous Ms. McGregor. How can we help you?" Armand said gallantly.

I laughed. "Call me Ainsley. And I need a couple of gifts for a white elephant party tonight."

He frowned.

This time Justin laughed. "It's where everyone brings a gift, they draw numbers, and you can trade the gifts a few times to get what you want. It's a fun thing a lot of Americans do at the holidays."

"Oh. Yes. Is this Shannon's party?" Armand asked.

"Yes. It is."

"She invited us," Justin said. "I just told him it was a party and didn't say what kind."

"Ahhhh. Well, be forewarned, it can be vicious sometimes. When there's a great gift, like these ornaments, people can get kind of feisty. The Christmas spirit goes right out the window."

They laughed.

"You want ornaments?"

I nodded. "Actually, I'm going to buy some for my tree, as well, and I want the pyramid twirly thing that has the carved dancing bears." They carefully boxed everything for me, and then Justin carried it to my car.

"Is everything okay?" I asked as he placed the items in the back of my SUV. I loved that everything was already gift-wrapped, though the bear pyramid was staying at my house.

"What do you mean?"

I stared at my feet. "I'm being nosy—never mind."

"It's okay. What are you talking about?" he asked as he shut the hatch door.

"I saw the two of you arguing earlier. I just wanted to make sure everything is all right. I mean, I just met you two, but I adore you both." It was true. There were people I met in life, who I find an instant kinship with—and I felt that way about these guys.

"My husband wants me to talk to the sheriff."

"Do you know something about—uh—Davy's case?" I almost called him Martin.

"Maybe. I'm not a big fan of law enforcement. And I really didn't want to get involved. I'm sure it's nothing."

I pursed my lips, as I lifted my head. "If you want to tell me, I can let my brother know, and I won't mention your name. I promise."

He frowned and then sighed. "I feel bad because I should have come forward earlier—if nothing else, just to help them with the timeline."

"I swear, I won't say a word about you. I'll just say I

overheard some guys talking, but I wasn't sure who they were."

"You'd do that for me?"

I nodded.

"It's not a big deal, or I would have come forward sooner. But the afternoon Davy was killed, I heard a woman in there with him. They were laughing and having a good old time. I didn't see who it was, though. Like I said, it's not much. But I thought it would be good if they knew a female had been with him."

No one but Rob had entered through the front. That meant it was a person who knew about the back entrance.

"Okay. Do you know what time that was?"

"I don't know maybe after four or so. We were unloading boxes for the booth. I didn't see anyone but it was definitely a woman's voice. I just remember thinking, I bet Davy's up to his shenanigans again."

That was right around the time of death. But I hadn't seen Justin in the footage, and I should have. "Were you walking on the main fairway?"

"No. Well I did, but then crossed behind because the entrance to our booth is in the back."

Interesting. There were other cameras, including the one on the back of my store. It could be that he had circumvented the one that faced the Santa house.

I wonder who else might have done that.

As I pulled into my drive, for the third time in a week,

there was someone at my house. Only, this time, it was Jake, who was on top of my roof without his shirt on.

"Oh. Lawd," as Shannon likes to say.

The man was hanging Christmas lights on my house.

"I'm confused," I whispered.

"Mrreooo." I interpreted that as George saying, "Me, too."

Swallowing hard, I pulled around Jake's truck and under the carport.

After letting George out in the fenced part of the backyard, I gathered my packages from the back of the SUV.

"Hey, Ains," Jake yelled down from the roof. "I'll be down in a minute. Do you like them?"

It was hard to see in the daytime, but he'd hung the multicolored lights I bought on sale after the holidays last year. The three snowmen and Santa's sleigh sat on my porch. He'd pulled everything out of the barn and put my lights up for me.

What is going on?

Still confused, I sat all my stuff down on the kitchen table and headed out to get the things I'd picked up from Armand and Justin.

Jake whistled "Jingle Bells" on the roof, and I swear I tried not to stare at those abs. But it was Jake, and they were oh so hawt. Did people even say hot like that anymore?

"Just need to do the ones on the side," he said. "And then you can tell me where you want your yard ornaments to go."

Why was he acting like things weren't horribly awkward between us?

George nudged me from behind, and I put the rest of the stuff in the house and then poured myself a glass of iced tea. I chugged it all in one gulp, and poured more. Whiskey might have been better, but there was a party later and I didn't want to go drunk.

I poured Jake a glass of tea and waited. Okay, I should have gone out and offered to help, but I wasn't sure I'd be able to stop gawking at him.

I'd just wanted to come home and relax. Take a hot bath and get ready for my not-date with Rob.

Maybe Jake's just being a good friend.

Greg probably mentioned I wanted to put my lights up and asked Jake to do it. Even though I'm perfectly capable of doing it myself. Well, I have an awful thing about heights, but if it meant my house looked cute—I'd do it.

"Ainsley," he said from the door. "I need you to tell me how you want to set up your snowmen and the sleigh with the presents."

I took a deep breath, and walked back out front.

"I was thinking one at each corner of the porch. And then the lighted sleigh and presents out in the front yard in the middle." Look at me acting like it's normal that a guy who isn't really speaking to me is putting up my Christmas décor.

"That's what I was thinking. I may have to run back to my house to get another extension cord. Depends on how far out you want the sleigh."

I pointed to a spot just beyond the flowerbeds that lined my sidewalk. This time of year, I had mums planted, even though I was allergic to them. They were hearty, colorful, and this far south would last through the holidays.

"That works. I have enough to put it there. And I can't do it today, but I'm lighting my trees along the road. I can do yours, as well. Mr. Harvey down the road is doing his. It'll look nice."

"Uh. Jake?"

"Yeah?"

My heart did what I called the Jake flip. That grin of his was stupid sexy.

"Why are you here? Did my brother ask you to do this?"

His head jerked back and he frowned. "Of course not. This is an early Christmas present for you."

I rubbed the bridge of my nose with my fingers. "I'm—I don't understand. You've been ignoring me for months while you were gone. And then things were super awkward—they still are. Now, you're putting lights up?"

"I'm sorry." He was so downtrodden, that I actually felt bad.

"For which part?"

"All of it," he said. "The emergency services training I was at was the most intense three months of my life. As in, I fell into bed every single night exhausted mentally and physically. They crammed two years of training into three months, for the emergency preparedness initiative. By the time I realized how much time had passed, I felt guilty that I hadn't talked to you—and I wanted to do it in person. Then there was this whole thing with…"

Wait, had he been seeing someone else? Bile rose in my throat.

"Your brother."

My head snapped up. "My brother?"

"Before I left, he told me that if I wasn't serious about you—like getting married serious, I needed to let you go."

I'm going to kill him. Like premeditated going to shoot him dead.

"And why would you listen to him?"

Jake's head dropped and he stared down at his boots. "I was in such a rush, and I had a lot to learn before the training even started—I couldn't make that sort of commitment right then. I mean, getting married is a big deal and we'd only been together for a couple of months."

Greg told him he had to marry me if he wanted to date me.

That had to be extenuating circumstances. I just needed an all-woman jury, preferably ones with nosy brothers. There wasn't a court in Texas that would convict me.

"You're right. It is. We hung out a lot, but we've been on exactly two dates, Jake. Have I ever mentioned marriage to you? Ever? Have I even mentioned that might be something I'd be interested in?"

"You're angry."

"Yes. I. Am. I'm an adult. I make decisions for myself, have been doing it for years. My mother would have said since the day I was born. She always thought I was too independent. Nobody has ever had great success telling me what I can and can't do. Just ask my idiot brother."

"You're really mad." He took a step back.

I probably did look like I had murder in my eyes. "I don't want to get married, Jake. Not right now, anyway. To anyone. Maybe down the road, but I'm married to my store right now. I'm focused on my career and I very much love my life the way it is."

That was the first time, in a long time, that statement was true.

"While I appreciate my brother is probably looking out for me in his own idiotic way, if you ever want to date me again you will discuss things with me. Do you understand?"

That last part may have come out more harshly than I meant. I'm known for having an even temper—but this was ridiculous.

"You're right. About everything." He held up his hands in surrender. "I've never been serious about any woman—except for you. And I just wanted to do right by you. It wasn't me making decisions for us, I just didn't know how to have this conversation. I like you a lot, Ainsley. More than I ever have anyone else—I should have just talked to you."

I nodded. "That's what people with successful relationships do. They discuss things. And they don't listen to stupid brothers who have no idea what they're talking about. Knowing Greg, he wants to marry me off, so he doesn't have to deal with me as much."

Jake chuckled.

"Why did you do all of this today?" I waved a hand toward my house.

"I wanted to show you how much I care about you. Every time I saw you—I just couldn't find the words."

Aww man. Anger. Gone. Just like that—in a poof of sincerity.

"Thank you." I bit my lip. "It's wonderful and I love it."

He gave me another grin. Dear, Lord, the man was gorgeous. He'd put his T-shirt back on, and I was able to focus on his face.

"Will you forgive me? Soon? I want to take you to the party tonight."

I sighed. "I already have a date."

His brow furrowed. "What?"

Chapter Twenty

To say things were tense inside Jake's truck as we pulled up to Shannon's party was an understatement. I'd taken him up on his offer to drive me. I'm not much of a drinker, but I planned on letting loose tonight. Within reason.

I mean, I'm still me.

My brother, Jake, Kane, and Mike would be there. There was only so much fun a girl could have when she had a bucket of guardians looking out for her. And I'd be taking my brother somewhere private and telling him exactly what I thought of him butting into my life.

"There's your date." Jake gritted his teeth when he said it.

Rob waited at the base of the stairs that led to Shannon's apartment above the shop. It was a balmy seventy degrees out tonight. Like Jake, he wore a button-down, dark jeans and boots. For guys in Texas, this was dressing up.

Rob was handsome. It's just—I had a thing for the guy sitting next to me.

"I thought you liked him," I said. Then I cleared my throat to keep from laughing. Maybe if he was jealous, he'd talk to me next time.

"He's a good guy. But I don't think you should be dating him. It's not like he's going to be around very long."

I couldn't take it anymore. I burst out laughing.

Jake turned toward me, a mask of confusion on his face.

"We came as friends. Just friends. He said he could tell I was interested in someone else."

We sat in silence for a minute.

"He's staring at us." Jake chuckled. "I'm sorry, Ains. I've been an idiot."

"Just remember the rule going forward."

"Talk to you first."

"Yep. Now help me out of this truck—my jeans are tight, and if I bend over too much I may cut myself in half."

He chuckled. "You're beautiful."

Whoa. A woman never tired of hearing that.

Rob smiled as we walked up. "So I take it you two made up?"

"We did." I grinned. "But you're my date tonight, and he's just going to have to suffer."

The two men shook hands.

"So it's like that?" Rob said.

"It is." Jake laughed. "Trust me, I deserve whatever is coming."

"I don't mind heading back to the caravan," Rob offered.

"Nonsense," I said. "You'll have the best view of the parade, right beside me. Plus, Shannon's cooking is incredible. You don't want to miss out."

"Come on," Jake interjected, "it'll be fun."

Rob threw his hands up in surrender. "I'm always up for a party."

AN HOUR LATER, I had a great buzz from the mulled wine and the parade began. There were kids on bikes decorated with Christmas ornaments. A couple of flatbeds with different holiday themes. Then there were some floats that the college kids had made and the marching band from the high school.

It was no Rose Parade but it was a fun night for the whole town and charming.

My cheeks were hot, and I was just thinking about grabbing water, when something flashed on the roof across the street.

One of the lighted floats went by and there on the ledge was Mary Beth. My chest tightened and my breath caught in my throat. Her body shook and she looked like she might fall any minute.

"Jake," I yelled and everyone at the party stopped. "Jumper." I started running. Thank God, I'd worn my flat-heeled boots. I was down the steps at Shannon's and trying to cross the very busy street when Jake caught up with me. While I was huffing and puffing, he was barely out of breath.

"Call my brother," I said as he rushed me across the parade run and through the barricade on the other side. Greg had left the party to be a part of the parade on the sheriff's float.

"What are you doing?"

"I'm climbing up there to stop Mary Beth. I think she's trying to kill herself."

"No," Jake said. "It's too dangerous."

"I'll be fine. Where is the entrance to the rooftop?"

The building was abandoned, but all the ones on Main

Street had large iron fire escapes. I ran around back, but didn't see it.

"I'm telling you, whatever she's doing, I probably have the best chance of stopping her. She's super ill and probably doesn't know what she's doing."

I stopped to catch my breath but only for a second. If she fell off that roof—I couldn't think about that.

"You find Greg and go do your fireman thing. Get one of those things for when people fall. Where is the darn fire escape?"

"There." Jake pointed toward the corner of the building. The stairs and the paint on the old store were black. "It's not safe. God knows the last time they were checked out."

"Well, if Mary Beth got up there, I can. Don't come after me. Or at least stay midway down. I don't want to spook her okay?"

"Ainsley, there are professionals who do this for a living. Your brother and I trained for situations like this."

I took a deep breath and closed my eyes. "I need you to trust me," I whispered as we were getting closer to the top. "Like I said, she's sick. She's probably running a high fever or has taken some meds and isn't thinking right. She needs a friendly face, or at least I would. I have to try."

"Okay. But I'm right here, and I'll call the emergency team. Just keep her talking?"

I nodded, and climbed over the ledge of the building. I moved slowly so as not to startle her.

"What are you doing here?" a voice said from behind me.

I turned to see Caroline holding a gun.

I did not see that coming.

Chapter Twenty-One

I'M NOT A big fan of guns, and I really, really don't like them when they are pointed at me. "Hi, Caroline," I squeaked. "Is everything okay?" She waved the end of the pistol at me, as in motioning me closer to Mary Beth on the ledge.

"Ainsley?" Mary Beth hiccupped a sob. "I'll jump, Caroline. Just don't hurt her. Please. She's a sweet girl and she hasn't done anything wrong."

"Except, she'll tell her brother that I held a gun on you." Caroline turned her focus on me. "She has to die. She killed him. I know she did."

Maybe it was the mulled wine, or the gun, but dizziness hit me and I had to grab the ledge. "Mary Beth, you need to get down from there," I croaked. "There are little children waiting for Santa. You're going to traumatize them for life."

"Stay where you are." Caroline's voice had a sinister tone.

"Whatever happened, killing Mary Beth isn't going to make it better," I said. There was movement behind Caroline, but she didn't see my brother or Lucy, who were on either side of her.

It was dark, but Lucy made a hand motion that looked like I needed to keep her talking.

"A life for a life," Caroline said. "It's in the Bible."

I'm pretty sure that's not how it went but now didn't seem the right time to correct her.

"Before we die," I said. "Can one of you explain what's going on? I assume this has to do with Martin."

"Martin?" Mary Beth asked. "Who's that?"

Way to go, Ainsley. "I meant, uh, Davy. Sorry. I'm nervous."

"Is that his real name?" Caroline asked.

"Yes."

"Everything really was a lie," she sniffed.

"Only the name. He had to protect himself from pretty bad folks. He had to become Davy. And he was a good man. His testimony put those bad guys away. I don't think he lied about his name or his past because he wanted to; it was to keep himself, and those around him, safe."

Caroline cleared her throat, and used her shirt sleeve to wipe her nose. "I always knew he was hiding something, but he was good to me. Treated me kindly. I've been in pretty messed-up relationships, but it wasn't like that with him. He was tender."

My brother made a hand motion and his deputies feathered out on both sides of the roof.

Thankfully, Caroline didn't seem to notice.

"I only met him once, but everyone who knew him says the same thing," I offered gently. "I wish I could have known him better."

Her arm straightened and she pointed the gun again. "He would have liked you. You're an intelligent young woman. And I don't want to kill you. I really don't. But she has to confess. She has to tell you what she did. I was drunk when she slipped. It took me a couple of days to remember. But she killed my Davy."

I swear my brother has ninja moves. He was only a few feet away from Caroline. Mary Beth had to see what was happening, as well, but she was smart enough not to say anything.

"Mary Beth, maybe you should tell me what happened." I turned away from Caroline and faced the other woman, who was even more wobbly than she had been before. I was prepared to jump and grab a leg if I had to, but I hoped it didn't come to that.

"I was there when Davy tripped," Mary Beth sobbed. "He cared about you, Caroline. I swear he did. He talked about you all the time. And you need to know, he never touched me, not in that way. He was a big flirt but you shouldn't be jealous."

"I don't care about any of that. I want to know why you killed him."

"I didn't. I told you that. When we'd been unloading for the festival, there was a big group of us who stopped to chat in the parking lot. He said we should come by and see the Santa house, that there was a secret entrance on the back. Then he texted us all to see where we were." She sobbed again and again, and then took a deep shuddering breath. "I'm so sorry, Caroline. You have no idea."

"No. You tell her what you did." Caroline stepped closer, and pointed the gun at Mary Beth.

"Don't hurt her," I said, stepping in front of the other woman. "I understand you're upset but you haven't hurt anyone yet. From what you're saying, it was Mary Beth who killed Davy."

"I didn't kill him," she wailed beside me. "It was an accident. I was gonna surprise him. I snuck in. He stood there facing the front doors, like he was waiting for someone. I jumped on to his back, just to play a joke. But he stumbled and fell on that stupid pole with me on top of him.

"At first, I didn't realize what was happening. I thought he was playing a joke and pretending to be dead. But then I went around the front of him—" The sobs started again.

"Tell her the rest," Caroline moaned, tears streaming down her cheeks. The gun dropped to her side and then popped back up. My brother went to grab it, and it went off. It all happened in slow motion. At least, it seemed like it. Something stung my shoulder.

My brother grabbed the gun before it hit the ground.

He started to move forward, but I shook my head.

Caroline was out of her mind with grief. I don't think she had any idea what was going on behind her, or that she no longer had the gun.

Mary Beth coughed and it rattled through her body. I had to get her off that ledge. "I pushed him hard, and he fell back into the chair. I remembered seeing on television that when someone has a pole in them. You leave it, and you call 911. But Davy wasn't breathing. And he had these three candy canes stuck in his mouth. And his face... It's just the most awful thing I've ever seen."

"Why didn't you call the police?" I asked.

"I grabbed Davy's phone but it was dead. I was running out the back for my phone, when I heard you and your friend. I peeked around the corner of the building—and you'd found him. I panicked. I ran to my car and just sat there for an hour, knowing the police would be coming for me any minute. But they didn't.

"I convinced myself that nobody would believe it was an accident. And with my past—you know four husbands—even though Davy and I weren't like that—I think I went crazy. Like, put it out of my mind that I wasn't the one who hurt him. It was...too much.

"I'm not proud of what I did. But I—my head is really messed up. It's not an excuse. I was sad and I'm not good with sad."

I'd heard stories about people just forgetting terrible things they'd done or trauma they'd experienced. I believed her.

She lifted her head to face Caroline. "I know you loved him. He was one of the best friends, besides you, that I ever had. That night on the River Walk, I was drunk and then everything came flooding back. But I couldn't tell if it was an awful nightmare or the truth."

"You said, 'I'm sorry, Davy,' in your sleep. You said you didn't mean to kill him but you did."

That explained the death stare earlier in the day.

"And however long I have left, I'm gonna have to live with what happened. It was a freak accident, but I—" She sobbed. "Caroline, if it will heal your sorrow, I will jump off this building. I mean it. Say the word. I'm not sure how I'm supposed to live with myself."

She wobbled again.

"No," Caroline shouted. "Don't jump. We'll figure it

out." She cried and held out her arms. "I was mad. I know you didn't mean to hurt him, and I can't lose both of you. But you had to tell them what happened."

"It's okay, hon," Mary Beth said. "You're right, people needed to know the truth."

Mary Beth stumbled. Her plump body falling backward.

We all screamed. I reached for her but she was propelled forward, right on top of an unsuspecting Caroline. Both women were laid out flat, but neither of them moved. I glanced over my shoulder to find Jake on a ladder. He'd been the one to push her off the ledge.

"You okay?" he asked as he climbed over the ledge and took me in his arms. My body shook hard. I wasn't sure how much longer my legs would hold me up.

I breathed in his soft woodsy scent, as his arms tightened around me.

"I will be."

He held me away for a few seconds, like he was checking me for injuries. He frowned. "Get a lift up here now," he yelled.

His shirt was wet and had red stains. "You got something on your shirt." I reached out and touched it and even in the dark of the roof I could tell it was blood.

"Jake, why are you bleeding? Did that bullet hit you?"

"Greg," Jake shouted.

I turned to see what was going on. Caroline and Mary Beth had sat up, and the deputies were trying to help them stand.

Then all heads turned toward Jake and me.

"Why is everyone looking at us?"

Jake cleared his throat. "Ainsley, you've been shot."

My head filled with cotton and my brain wouldn't function. "No. I'm fine."

I glanced down to find blood spreading across my chest. "Darn. I really liked this shirt."

And then everything went black.

Chapter Twenty-Two

A WEEK LATER, everyone from the shop and a few people from the festival, gathered out at my house. Jake had gone overboard with the decorations, and had added a couple of lighted pine trees to my front yard. I didn't have the heart to tell him I was allergic.

The backyard looked like a winter wonderland. He'd wrapped the trees lining my property. He'd been proud of himself, and I had to admit it was charming.

He'd been sleeping on my couch every night since I was shot. Every morning I woke up to a full breakfast, and every night there was dinner. The townsfolk had delivered so much food. He'd frozen a lot of it and sorted it in the freezer. But I never lacked for a meal.

Everyone thought I was nuts for throwing a party the week after I'd been shot. But the bullet had gone through my shoulder, in what my brother called a through and through.

I had to stay in the hospital for a night but they let me go home the next day and said to take it easy. I did for a whole day, and then George and I were bored. No one at the shop would let me work. We stayed in the back and I caught up on a lot of paperwork for a few hours and then I'd go home and watch Hallmark movies. It hasn't been as big of a struggle as everyone keeps making it out to be. I've never been mother-hen'd so much.

Mrs. Whedon and Shannon had done all the holiday decorating on the inside of the house and had provided a lot of the side dishes for tonight. The older woman said it was to thank me for taking her home most nights and buying her dinner, but I'd enjoyed hanging out with her. She'd lived quite the life before coming to Sweet River and had great stories she shared with me and Shannon.

George was on the back deck with his Santa hat, and my brother Greg worked the large grill he and Jake had brought over from his house. Everyone from the shop was there, along with the gang from the carnival, and Armand and Justin.

I never did tell Greg what Justin had heard. It didn't seem necessary, now that we knew the truth. For that, I had received his and Armand's eternal gratitude. I planned on making a trip to their shop soon to pick up more inventory. A road trip that Jake wanted to go on. There was a restaurant in Austin he wanted to take me to that served breakfast all day long. Breakfast food is my favorite.

Who am I kidding? I like all food. I just have a special kind of love for pancakes and French toast. And um, crepes and cheese blintzes.

"What are you thinking about?" Shannon asked.

"Things are good," I said. Jake handed Greg a tray to put the burgers on. It wasn't a very Christmassy main meal, but everyone would have enough of that kind of food over the next few weeks. We had beef, turkey, and black bean burgers.

And folks had brought tons of sides and desserts, even

though I said they didn't have to.

"I'm not sure I've ever seen you smile so much as you have the last week." Shannon smirked. "Did you forget you'd been shot?"

It was a busy time for Jake and me, but we'd found quiet moments to be together. It was relaxed and fun like it had been a few months ago, and I was happy about that. And I'd even caught him watching Hallmark movies when I wasn't even home yet. I liked that about him.

I'd been through enough failed relationships to know it took time and courage to create a great one. Something like the trust Shannon and Mike or the adorable Don and Peggy.

Those two were still grieving the loss of their friend.

"He never takes his eyes off you when he's around."

I lifted my head to find she was right. Even as he held the tray, he was grinning at me.

"Like I said, life is good."

"Have you heard anything about Mary Beth?"

"She's still in the hospital. Doctors say it'll be another few weeks." She had pneumonia, which was why she'd been so sick. Caroline had been stuck to her side like glue. The two had made up.

I'd refused to press charges against Caroline. Mainly, because they weren't really sure if she or Greg accidentally pulled the trigger. It happened as he took the gun from her.

She didn't mean for that gun to go off. I don't think she even knew when it happened.

Caroline had come to see me at the shop a few days ago. She apologized profusely and cried. She actually wanted me to press charges. She felt she deserved it, which made me even more determined not to do it, much to my brother's chagrin. I forgave her.

When I asked how things were going with Mary Beth, she explained that they were both all alone in the world, and Davy/Martin would want them to take care of each other. It was their way of honoring him.

In fact, Don and Peggy were waiting to do Martin/Davy's memorial, until Mary Beth was well enough to attend.

When she was better, Mary Beth would be arrested for obstruction of justice. Her lawyer had already worked out a deal for community service. It wasn't exactly legal what they'd done, but the judge here in town was fair and liked to do things his way.

It was for the best.

My brother wasn't happy but he was grateful the bullet hadn't been closer to my heart. Two inches lower, and I wouldn't be here.

Christmas tunes played over the speakers Jake had set up. Everyone sat in a big circle around the fire Jake and Greg had built. My brother had been extra nice this past week.

I may have given him a piece of my mind, and then some, when he'd come to see me at the hospital. I blamed the painkillers they'd given me but I'd meant every word.

I made him hold up a hand and take an oath that he would never butt into my relationships again. And he promised. Knowing he was the kind of man who kept promises, I decided that was good enough. But I still managed to give him the stink eye when he chanced looking at me.

Rob and his crew waved. They were coming back for the Valentine's festival in February. I was looking forward to that. He'd witnessed—along with a lot of my friends, and most of the parade—what had happened. They couldn't hear us, but they'd seen it.

"Ainsley, I need to talk to you." Mrs. Whedon wagged a finger at me from the doorway to my kitchen.

I squeezed Shannon's arm. "I better go see what she wants."

I followed the elderly woman, who was dressed in an avocado-green pantsuit with sequined Christmas trees all over it. On most people, it would be garish, but it worked for her.

Someday, I'd be brave enough to ask why she always wore green.

She led me into the living room. "I know we're doing the Santa gifts later, but I didn't want to embarrass folks, since my gift is probably better than what they're giving."

Coughing into my hand, to keep from laughing, I cleared my throat. "Thank you."

"That's from me." She pointed to a huge box, as in it was as big as she was. "You're one of the good people in the world, and you deserve happiness. Now, open your gift."

I already knew what she was giving me, but maybe she'd forgotten she told me. However, the box was extra-large.

I opened the gift. It wasn't a blanket, it was an antique hope chest. "Had to get your brother to help me wrap it." The idea of my brother wrapping anything made me giggle, especially with Mrs. Whedon over his shoulder.

"It's gorgeous, but I don't understand."

I glanced up to find her eyes teary.

"You're okay aren't you?" *Please don't let her be dying. I can't take it.* She was a fiery hornets' nest most days, but I'd grown to love her. I couldn't imagine the world without her.

"Of course I'm okay. I'm going to outlive you all."

Relieved, I laughed. "That's true."

"You're the closest thing to family I have. And I wanted you to start your new life with that boy knowing that you're loved. You don't have your grandmother or your momma, who loved you dearly. And I want you to know I do too."

Water fell down my cheeks, at a surprising rate.

"Open it," she said.

Inside the large chest was the blanket, and throw pillows to match, along with an entire set of lovely white china, with lacy-gold filigree around it. I recognized the pattern as one I'd seen in antique stores. It was way too pricey for me to buy myself.

"It's too much." I might have sobbed. And then I stood and hugged her.

She patted my back. "Nonsense. You're family now. When you saved those women last week, I had a hard think about how I'd feel if we lost you. Turns out I love you like my own. You can call me grandma if you want. Even in public. I've never said that to anyone. But if I had a granddaughter, I would hope she was as brave, thoughtful, and intelligent as you."

A large frog lodged in my throat and speaking was impossible.

I got a grandma for Christmas. I squeezed her tight.

"Now. Now. I'm old and brittle—don't hug me too hard." But she pulled me in tighter and kissed the top of my head. Then she gently shoved me away from her. "Enough of that. You need to fix up your makeup, and get back out there. You've got a party to throw."

Then she was off. I started laughing, tears streaming down my face.

After running upstairs and reapplying my makeup, I headed back down to find Lily and Jeff waiting for me by the tree in my living room.

"Hey, I didn't expect you guys to make it tonight."

Jeff was beaming. "It's not that far to come back and we wanted to let you know in person about Terry and his mom."

Lily had been keeping me informed via text, but I hadn't heard the latest.

We sat down on the sofa.

"Is everything okay?"

Lily nodded. "Terry is doing great. He and my brother are like best friends now, and we go to see his mom twice a day."

"Poor little guy. How is she? Have you guys heard anything?"

"We visited her, before we drove here. She's doing a lot better," Lily said. "Our parents wouldn't tell us what was going on, but it turns out she has M.S. She'd been misdiagnosed by her last doctor. Jeff's dad says it's an easy thing to miss if the right tests aren't run."

Oh, no. That was pretty serious. "How much longer will she be in the hospital?"

"She'll be able to spend Christmas with Terry at our house." Lily squeezed her hands together. "My mom is going crazy with the decorating and trying to create the perfect holiday fantasy. It's one of the reasons we're here tonight. I had to get away from the crazy. Mom is the sweetest, but she's like a drill sergeant and a perfectionist."

My mom had been the same way when she was alive.

"Anyway, she's responding to the treatments and getting stronger every day. There's not a cure for what she has, but my dad says they have ways of managing it and she's in the early stages."

Well, at least there was that. Still, my heart hurt for that little boy and his mom. They had a tough road ahead.

"Get this, before she got sick, she was a teacher," Lily added. "When her teacher friends in Dallas found out what happened, they rallied around her. She never told any of them what was wrong. Just said she needed some time off. Once she's better, she and Terry will be able to move in with one of them. But they are looking at houses in Sweet River. They love it here so much."

"Awwww. That's great news." I sniffed. I was not going to cry again. "Thank you both for everything you've done. It feels like we had a part in a holiday miracle."

"We feel the same way."

Lily stood. "We don't want to keep you. I know you have a lot of guests out there. We just thought you'd like an update."

"I'd hug you both, but I can only lift one arm."

Lily threw her arms around me and gently squeezed, and Jeff threw his arms around the both of us.

"We might be your students, but we're always going to be your friends, Ms. McGregor," Lily said.

They let go.

"You two are something else. Now go eat, and stay away from the mulled wine. You won't be able to drive home."

They laughed.

As I followed them out the back door, Jake was there holding a plate with a burger and a bite of every single side. He handed it to me. It was like he knew me or something.

"Is everything okay? You were gone a long time."

I glanced out over my friends enjoying themselves and maybe being loud and crazy. I loved it.

"I'm the luckiest woman in the world," I said as he put his arm around me.

I lifted my head to find him smiling at me.

Yep. Luckiest woman in the world.

The End

Want more? Check out Ainsley's first adventure in *A Case for the Winemaker*!

Join Tule Publishing's newsletter for more great reads and weekly deals!

If you enjoyed *A Case for the Toy Maker,*
you'll love the next book in….

The Ainsley McGregor series

Book 1: *A Case for the Winemaker*

Book 2: *A Case for the Yarn Maker*

Book 3: *A Case for the Toy Maker*

Book 4: *A Case for the Candlemaker
Coming in Feburary 2021!*

Available now at your favorite online retailer!

About the Author

Bestselling and award-winning author Candace Havens has had more than thirty novels published. She is one of the nation's leading entertainment journalists and has interviewed countless celebrities from George Clooney to Chris Pratt. She does film reviews on Hawkeye in the Morning on 96.3 KSCS.

Thank you for reading

A Case for the Toy Maker

If you enjoyed this book, you can find more from all our great authors at TulePublishing.com, or from your favorite online retailer.

Made in the USA
Monee, IL
26 August 2021